Stories of the
Eastern Shoshone

In Gratitude for the Preservation of these Stories: Contributors
These *Shoshone Stories* were first told to Ake Hulktranz by John and
Debra Trehero
Geraldine Hulktranz, Ake's wife, transcribed again and shared them with Wind
River Historians and Children
Illustrations were drawn by Children of the Wind River (Art classes of George
Abeyta and Wendy Elias)
John Washakie assisted in translations
Rock Art Photography, digitization, and design, and cover design contributed
by Jim Stewart

Editing and Printing: Mortimore Publishing, Lander, Wyoming
Copyright November 2009
ISBN   978-0-9721352-3-8

+

Library of Congress in Publication Data
Hulktranz, Ake and Geraldine
Shoshone Stories
Illustrated by Children of the Wind River
Consultant John Washakie
Rock Art Photography & Cover James Stewart
Editor; Mortimore Publishing, Lander, Wyoming
Copyright November 2009
ISBN: 978-0-9721352-3-8

Mortimore Publishing, P. Trautman
805 Mortimore Lane
Lander, Wyoming 82520 USA

W.H. Jackson photograph of Chief Washakie's Council Lodge on Willow Creek, South Pass, September 1870. Jackson was part of the Hayden expedition surveying the west. *Photograph Courtesy of the National Archives.*

Shoshone Stories

There is a great wealth of stories and legends saved among American Indians. Some of them are only partly known today, others have been written for posterity in a more complete fashion, and have found their way into well-known reference works. It is wonderful to note how many Stories there still are among the people of today and are still being told around campfires. Many of them are directed to the children. In this book of Shoshone Stories, the main emphasis is on narratives that catch the young imagination.

The folk stories were told by wise old people to the Indian youngsters before they retired for the night. The raconteurs were sometimes older relatives, such as a grandfather or a grandmother, sometimes more "professional" historians who were highly regarded for their story telling. Such favoured persons were also praised for their knowledge of Shoshone past events and the occurrence of spirits and other supernatural beings. Many of them were "medicine men," that is, Indian doctors and healers. Some of them were very well known, for example John Trehero, or "Rainbow" (parókogare), and Tudy Roberts. Another highly praised storyteller was Enga Shoyo, who could recite long stories about people and spirits of the past.

The Authors of the stories say the Shoshone people have always lived in Wyoming and neighbouring states. The storyteller and medicine man John Trehero, told me many of the stories that I have related in this book(with a twinkle in his eyes). We believe the reader will agree that many parallels can be found in cultures all over the world.

With many blessings, Åke and Geraldine Hultkrantz, February 2003 Stockholm, Sweden

Post script by Geraldine Hultkrantz:
In 1983 I had the privilege to accompany my husband Ake to Fort Washakie, and to meet John Trehero in the hospital in Lander for the last time. He was then ninety-nine years old and although he was very ill, his great sense of humour prevailed. It has given me great joy to translate and compile these stories from my husband's notes, made from 1948 until well into the 1970's. With kindest regards, Geraldine

John Trehero [Rainbow] *Parókogare*
Ake *Hultkrantz Photograph*

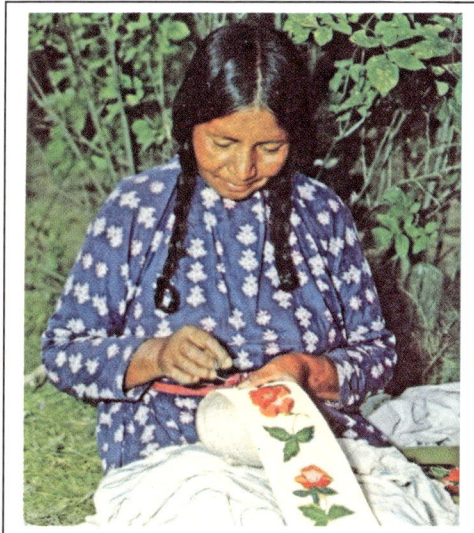

Deborah Trehero *Puyep*
Ake Hultkrantz photograph

5

Table of Contents

Photo Illustrations are Rock Art (petroglyphs) from the Wind River Valley, Big Horn Basin, and Green River Basin courtesy of Jim Stewart, Lander, Wyoming. Current dating processes estimate some area petroglyphs are possibly up to 6,500 plus years old, or older, pre-dating the tribes who currently inhabit the Wind River Valley. However, on the other hand, some date as recent as possibly the mid to late 19th Century, and are thus possibly of Shoshone, Arapaho, Sioux, Crow, and Blackfoot.

The Childrens' Art works are submitted by courtesy of children of the Warm Valley, Wind River Country. The pictures were drawn in the school art classes of George Abeyta and Wendy Elias. The artists are:
"How Long the Winter Should Last" Andrea H.
"Creation Tales" Jeston Edino
"Wolf and Coyote Creating the World" Kailyn Washakie
"Story of Cottontail" Brilee Forton, Erin Sparkman, & Sydney Polson.
"Story of Wolf &Coyote", Sady Cunningham

Introduction

The telling of stories was called *náreguyap:* but the storytellers, *náreguinar,* do not own the stories. "Anybody could tell a story who knew a story." However, it was said about Cyrus Shongutsie, that he could not tell a story well. "He can't tell a story though." "Some add a lot to the story, to make it sound worse – but I tell the way I learned it" maintained John Trehero. He got his stories from the father of his wife, Deborah, also known as *Puyep,* and from his grandmother – most of the Coyote stories are from her. He complained that in his days the Shoshone youngsters did not bother about the stories, they did not listen to them and they considered John a crazy man when he wanted to tell stories. There were many different kinds of stories and the Coyote, *nimírika,* (cannibal or monster) stories distinguished themselves from the others.

All the stories that John Trehero had heard from the old people were considered to be true, and they were looked upon as enacted events that had happened in the old days "when Coyote ruled over the world." The old folk told these stories in the evenings. "They have to quit before midnight because they want to say *pasadasakogen,* that is, we want it warm tomorrow." The listeners were grown ups and children, mostly children. "All stories are supposed to be told to kids." The stories were intended to be entertaining, amusing or thrilling. The children were often frightened, for example by the *nïmïrika* "monster" stories. At the same time the stories were educational: children should keep quiet and be calm, otherwise a monster or troll could appear. After telling a story about *nïmïrika* (see Chapter 5) John commented: "That story will keep boys at home, and prevent them from making much noise."

An old woman, *Táivowui* "eyes like white man," who died in 1917 at the age of 95 years maintained that "Folks who have no grandparents don´t get stories, but we had grandparents, we heard them and our parents tell stories. Kids are taught stories in the evening, to keep them quiet."

Helen Wesaw (*née* Hill, wife of Tom Wesaw) said that one would get ill if the stories were told during the day and moreover no stories were to be told during summertime. However, George Wesaw (son of Tom) said that certain stories could be told in the summer and others in the winter. But if winter stories were told in the summer it could result in a very heavy snowfall.[1]
He went on to say that Coyote stories should not be told before the end of October, when the snow came, otherwise one could get snowed in.

Concerning time: the famous wintercounts drawn on blankets were not made by the Shoshone, but were, for example, made by the Crow. The Shoshone

7

could read them though as John Trehero demonstrated deftly by interpreting the pictures in a book that illustrated a wintercount.When it came to distances they measured in *páiygwáwic,* "sleeps". One sleep was approximately 20 miles.

The months essentially followed the phases of the Moon so that the Shoshone "months" slowly turned into the months of the white man. John Trehero said that when he was a young man he was the tribe's interpreter and that he worked eight hours a day for four years together with Dr. Roberts[2] translating the Gospel into Shoshone.

The Shoshone months are as follows:
a. *ójinmea* ("cold month"), parts of January and February.
b. *bó:sij* ("half spring, half winter"), February to March.
c. *ñeimea* ("windy moon"), last part of March.
d. *išaró:a* ("Coyote's having pups-moon"), April.
e. *bú:huimea pu´:hidakómbï?* ("Spring month, brings the green leaves down"), May.
f. *yú:aiwöa* ("warm moons"), June, July, August.
g. *nágara:ts* ("half warm, half cold"), September.
h. *só:gorihamea* ("deer moon,"the deer run to meet the other sex), October.
i. *teimea* ("little moon," also called "deer season"), November.
j. *Píamea* ("big moon"), December.

Winter signs: when the geese and ducks fly south, it means a hard winter will prevail. "When the buffalo used to be here – that was before I was born," said John Trehero, "they went from these mountains to where the salt sage is in the prairies. If it was going to be a hard winter, they wandered on to the Pavilion country where it was not so windy."

Folklore concerning the moon and stars: the moon was used to predict weather forecasts, for example when the half moon was lying down it meant stormy and cold weather. When the crescent was turned to the left it meant hot weather.
The "Big Dipper" was called by the Shoshone "jack rabbits" (see story in the Creation Stories). Using the big dipper one could tell the time of the year.[3]

Notes on Introduction

1. Å.H. wrote these words on the 25th September, 1948 and says that he could not fully tell the stories that George Wesaw told him because it was neither summer nor winter just then. So he decided to relate certain characteristics from the stories as a caution in order not to provoke any trouble.
2. Dr. Roberts was a Doctor of Divinity, a very correct man who served as a missionary at Fort Washakie until his death in 1949.
3. In summertime the spire points upwards, in the Autumn it points to the left. In the winter it points downwards and in the spring it points to the right.

Please note that all the stories recounted here are from John Trehero unless otherwise stated.

Chief Washakie's camp on Willow Creek, South Pass, photographed by W. H. Jackson September 1870, with Hayden Survey Expedition. *Photograph Courtesey of National Archives.*

Chapter 1
Creation Stories

Before the white men were here, a story was told that two boys went all over the world in different directions and then they met up again. The two brothers were hunting up in the mountains and in the night one of them dreamt that the claws of an eagle killed his brother. (This happened later on). The great eagle (Pía Guina) took the dreaming boy between his claws and flew away. He saw the heavenly spirit. Then he saw smoke somewhere. He flew toward the smoke and when he arrived there an old lady appeared who gave him food, and told him to make a raft so that he could fly. She was the mother of the great eagle, and she killed people everywhere. Then the boy floated away and was attacked by a water giant, *pandzóavits,* and he had to fight for several days. The two boys met him and helped him up into a tree that was impossible for the water giant to climb. It nearly managed to reach him but he kicked at it and it fell down in the water again.[1]

A similar story recounts that two men (maybe the two boys) were out walking through a dark country, where, whenever an owl hooted, a flash of lightening lit up everything and they could see the dangers, for example over places where there were rattlesnakes. In the beginning someone had talked about the dangers "but don´t be afraid!" Cannibal giants could tickle you but also kill you if you laughed; a big mosquito who could twist its head around was perhaps a man but he could not laugh, so he cut a hole for his mouth. That is why people have mouths. In the old days they could only smell, but they had teeth in their mouths.

Animals and birds were people at one time. They have colours – they like to paint themselves, just like the Indians do.

Concerning Wolf and Coyote John Trehero said first of all that they both were the same as the devil. But is really Wolf and Coyote the same person? "No," said John, "Wolf is a trickster just as Coyote is. Wolf is some kind of a spirit that God made himself, and so is Coyote – they call themselves brothers. God created Wolf and Coyote, they are spirits still living. My own belief is that they are some kind of spirits sent by God to make the world. The way that Wolf and Coyote created the wild game sounds like true," said John, "but I don´t know how true it is."

Guardian Spirits and the Supreme Being

Every man has a guardian spirit who protects him from all dangers. God gave us this guardian spirit that came to us at birth and leaves us at death. It follows the soul, *múgua,* to the Creator and delivers her to him. The soul dwells between the eyes: "it is a vital spark of a heavenly flame." The *múgua* is also the personality, but it is not the self or ego, – self is breath, the breath of life. *Múgua* is a very vital, delicate thing, similar to a thin thread. If something happened in the body the *múgua* would leave the body immediately. For instance if someone died then the *múgua* would leave the body and return to the Great Spirit who had given birth to man (i.e. he is the Creator). No one had any knowledge of what actually happened when the *múgua* left the body, not even today. There were no dangers on the way to the kingdom of death, but nobody knew where this kingdom was situated. If the *múgua* is strong then it doesn't matter how much the body is shot at, it would still remain intact. In old times of war warriors could take many bullets, so they must have had several *múguas!*

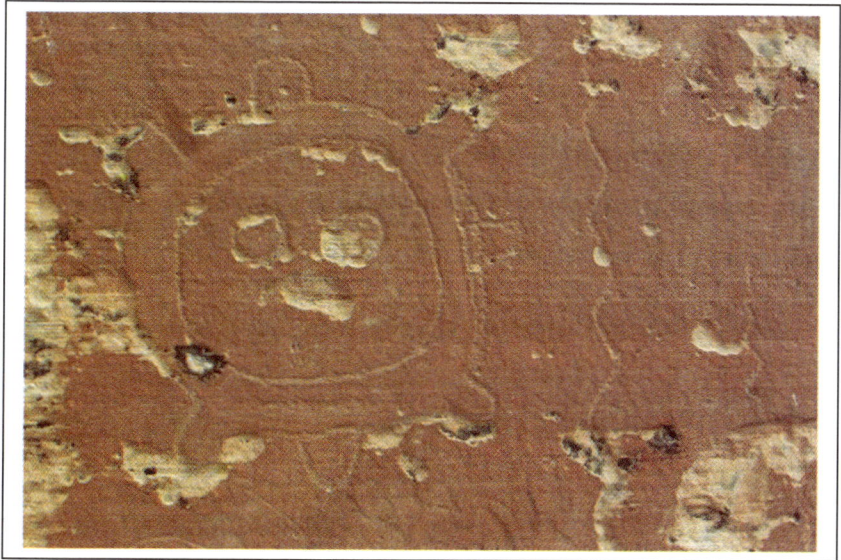

Certain people are believed to be superhuman and when they grow up they are intelligent and are more capable than others; they can cure sick people. Thus they are born with power (superhuman beings), or they can acquire power through the Sun Dance or at Medicine Butte. For example: a constantly sick man went to Medicine Butte in order that he may possibly be cured and then would be able to cure people himself. There were two categories of medicine men, but they all prayed for power through visions before carrying out their curing. They believed in one God. God created the sun so that all creatures on earth may see everything. The moon has the same function as the Sun. Probably God has also created the stars. The thunder is controlled by the thunderbird, = *túpísi hútchu,* = brown bird. The lightening is controlled by a bird that has a red spot; when it shakes you see the lightening.

11

The Sun and the Moon

Concerning the relationship between God and the sun, John Trehero says
"we don't know, but they claim that the sun might be God himself, looking
over the world every day." If the sun shines: "that's his [God's] power in his
light." Every morning when the sun rises "it looks as if the sun is going
round, spinning, very fast, and in one way. It doesn't hurt your eyes to look
at it; it is like looking at the moon. God shows himself even in the moon and
in fire."
The Medicine man, Valentine Cody could make rain: he prayed for rain to a
cloud that nobody could see when the sky was quite blue. Soon a large cloud
appeared, a puff of wind touched the Sun Dance Lodge, and a large raindrop
fell. Two to three drops of rain was enough to cool off the body.

How Wolf and Coyote Created People

A long time ago before there were people here Wolf said to Coyote: "I want
to get people in this world. Could we come up with people ourselves? And
how shall we make them?" – "Well, Brother," replied Coyote, "there is only
one way, and that is to make two women, one for you and one for me." –
"That's all right," said Wolf. "And how shall the babies come? Shall they
come from the thumb, or from the little finger?" – "Coyote replied: "No,
they shall come this way," and he put his right index finger between his left
thumb and his index finger;" Wolf said: "well, let me see what you mean." –
Coyote went to his woman and did to her what he had suggested with his
fingers. One morning sometime afterwards Coyote's wife came out with a
big stomach that hung in front of her. "Look," said Wolf's wife to her
husband, "your brother's wife has a big belly. How can that be?" Wolf came
out and saw the woman's stomach and then said: "I'll ask Coyote about it."
Shortly afterwards Wolf and Coyote went out hunting, and then Wolf asked
Coyote: "your wife has a big belly: how did you make it?" – "I did this said
Coyote and showed with his fingers what he had done. "And now there will
be children coming." –"How did you feel?" asked Wolf. "Pretty good!"
answered Coyote. – "I will do the same," said Wolf. – When he returned
home after the hunt he went to his wife; and soon she also came out with a
large stomach, and gave birth to a child. "Didn't you feel good," asked
Coyote. – "I felt pretty good," answered Wolf. "That's the way all people
shall have it." Coyote had a son, and Wolf had a daughter and they were
married later on. "Well," said Wolf, "we got our tribe started now." And that
is how people were created. Wolf and Coyote also created a male and a
female for all types of wild animals: two elks, two bears and so on. In this
way the birds were also created.

How Long the Winter Should Last
By Kailyn Washakie

How Long the Winter Should Last

Wolf said to Coyote, fooling him; "We better have winter the whole year round, twelve moons." Coyote went to the birds and the frogs and said: "How are you people? Let us see how we will have the seasons and the weather. Well, I think that we better have winter twelve moons and call it one year." But then the robin piped up: "No, that's too long a winter for birds and for water animals, that's no good." Then Coyote asked: "Who else has something to say?" Frog said: "I think that only four moons is good enough." "Well," said Coyote, "you people asking for four moons could have it, but I myself want twelve moons." So he went away and made a camp along the shore of a lake up in the mountains. It started to snow and the snow fell day and night non-stop. Coyote lay there for four moons. Then a spider went up to him and crawled up his arm. "Where do you come from?" asked Coyote – "green grass down there, " replied the spider. "Why did you come?" said Coyote – "I came over the mountains on the snow to see how you are getting along." "I´ll go with you," said Coyote. He wrapped his legs with pieces of bark like leggings, threw a buffalo hide over his shoulders, put on a belt and the next morning he and the spider went off. It was still snowing when they left. They crossed the mountains and came to a stream, where there was green grass, and it was warm and pleasant like a summer´s day. Some frogs in a pool said to Coyote: "Aren't you sorry that you made it so hard on yourself?" – "Where is Brother Wolf?" asked

13

Coyote. – "He is hunting over there, next to the mountains," answered the frogs. –"He fooled me," said Coyote; "he told me what to say, so we had better call him a big liar, *Ižápö.*" Coyote now went to the Wolf and said: "From now on we will have a winter of four moons." After telling this story John Trehero said, "it seems like its true, for there are four winter months – November, December, January and February."

How the Mosquito Got its Present Size

"The Mother of mosquitoes" walked up the valley with her children in a sack. In those days the mosquitoes were as big as blackbirds and they sucked people's blood and killed them in a short time. Their mother carried them in a sack so that nobody would notice them and when they arrived in a large Indian village she undid the sack so that they could go out and eat. In that way village after village was devastated. "They cleaned out the valley." They had now arrived at the fourth camp in the valley. It lay by the river. Before they arrived to eat up the people there a hunter had left the camp to go hunting for antelope. On his return he found all the inhabitants dead, the mosquitoes had killed them all. He hurried to the next camp that was Wolf and Coyote's camp and said "Mother mosquito and her children are coming here and they will kill everybody. They are as big as blackbirds with long bills and they clean the camps out." Coyote said: "I will go out and announce that people gather together so that we can get somebody with quiet wings that the mosquitoes can't see." When everyone was there Wolf and Coyote said to the Sagechicken: "You are grey, so they won't see you very well, let's see if you can do it." Sagechicken flew up but he made too much noise. Then they tried with Raven, but he was also too noisy. It was the same for Eagle and Woodpecker. However, the owl, *sí:wako,* flew very quietly. "Oh yes," said Wolf and Coyote, "this is the man who can do it." Then Coyote said to the owl: "When you go there take this string and sew up the sack so that the mosquitoes can't get out. As soon as you get that sack tied up we can charge on them." The owl took the string and flew away. Coyote said to the other animals: "you ought to have sticks with you to kill with." The mother of the mosquitoes wandered into the camp and said to her children: "Now, you kids keep quiet and you will soon have something to eat. I want you to get filled up with blood, so that you won't be crying for food. We are coming to a big camp now." The owl flew down quietly and sewed up the sack really well so that it couldn't be opened. Then he flew up into the air and all the animals rushed down the slope armed with sticks. They killed the mosquito mother and then the children. "The Coyote said: "I guess we got them all killed." But there was a small mosquito that hadn't been killed. It bit Coyote under his chin. Coyote said, "that's the way they are going to be, small ones, so they can't kill anybody," and that's how it turned out.

14

How the Animals Were Created

Before Coyote and Wolf created their wives, they started out for the mountains. Wolf was alone first and he created all the game. Coyote came into this world the same way that Wolf did. He said, "Brother, where did you get that game?" Wolf said, "I got it in this hole in the mountains." – "Well," said Coyote: "If you don´t plan to keep it all for yourself, can I get up there?" – "No," said Wolf, "I want to keep it for myself." – "No, Brother, said Coyote, your idea is not good." So they went on arguing but finally Wolf let him go to the mountains. He went up there, and opened the cave, and caught one of the animals. He looked at it and said, "Well, that's the way my brother did, he closed their mouths, and eyes, nose and ears. I'll open them so that they can live as animals should live, and I will let them loose, and then men can have more fun in hunting." So he opened the deer's mouth, eyes, nose and ears, and said, "that's the way I like to see them. All you animals can go now and live where you want to live." – Wolf looked up to the mountains. "Well," he said, "I have to work hard now to get my meat; these animals will be able to smell now and that will make it hard to hunt." Coyote came back. "Oh Brother," he said, "I have a nice deer, it will taste like soup! Your deer had no taste to it, but my deer will be tasty.

15

Chapter 2
Astral Stories

The Big Dipper (called the White Jackrabbits by the Shoshone)

Four jackrabbits were travelling north. "Now," they said, "there are four of us here, and we are going to find out who lives here and who lives there." They travelled and travelled, and travelled to the north, and met all kinds of animals, and asked them how far it was to the coldest place. Finally they met a bear as white as snow, and asked him, "How far is it from here to the coldest country?" – "Why do you ask me about the coldest country?" said the bear. "You are in the coldest country now. If you keep on travelling, they will call you the four jackrabbits in the sky." They kept going, going, going and they never met anybody. And where the earth and the sky came together they climbed into the sky. The white bear saw them in the north and said, "I guess we have to call them **the White Jackrabbits** (*tóšakamone?*)."

Orion – The Three Mountain Sheep

There was a small bat and a big bat. One day they were hunting in the mountains. They were looking for mountain sheep, but the little bat spied them first. In those days the mountain sheep used to live in the deserts like antelopes do. The little bat saw them now, a family of three sheep, the father, mother and a little lamb.' The big bat [2] told the little bat not to scare them away, so they would not go so high up in the sky where nobody could kill them. But the little bat said, "You stay here at this big gap, and don´t let

16

them go up into the mountains – if they do we'll lose them. I am going out into the desert to see if I can catch the leader of the mountain sheep. You better be careful –they are pretty smart, and if we miss them they will leave the prairies and go to live in the high mountains." "All right," the big bat said, "I will sneak in there and see what I can do." The little bat went down to the desert. The little mountain lamb said, "Father, somebody is here, it looks like a bat." – "Well," the father said, "let's get out of here, we are not here for his sake." They carried on up towards the mountains. The big bat, which was supposed to watch the gap, took a nap, so that the mountain sheep passed him. When he woke up, he saw their tracks. The little bat followed the tracks to find out if his brother had stopped the sheep. But the big bat had not, and the little bat got very mad at him. "Oh," he said, "that big black mouse, he let them pass, and now they are up in the sky. That's why the mountain sheep are way up high."[3]

The Story of Cottontail

Sydney Polson

17

The Story of Cottontail – *távuᵃ tzi*

Cottontail went around to different animals asking them what they thought about his plan to kill the sun. Coyote said to him, "Cottontail, I don't think that you could do it. And I don't know what you will get out of it. Why do you want to do it?" "Oh," Cottontail replied, "when the sun is shining it gets too hot, and I get too lazy. I don't get enough to eat in the daytime." Coyote said, "You better not try it. You can't do it. It's a pretty hard thing for one person to fight the sun." "I'll show you that I can do it," said Cottontail. "I will kill the sun, and it will be dark." "No," said Coyote, "I know that you can't kill him. The closer you get to him the more you will get burnt." "Well, I am going to show you," said Cottontail. "How long will it take you to get up there?" inquired Coyote. "Not very long, I am a fast runner," said Cottontail. Early the next morning he started out, and loped and loped and loped. He climbed a big mountain, and night fell. "Well," he said, "It looks pretty close from here. I am tired, I have loped all day, so I will sleep here." Next morning he loped again and reached further up the mountain, and it was getting hot. All at once he saw a sunbeam come down. It burned the back of his neck, and it turned yellow. He tried to fight the sunbeam, but he had nothing to fight with, and his feet got burnt and also turned yellow. "Well!" he said, "they told me that I could not do it." So he started running down and finally came to where the animals were. Wolf said, "We told you that you couldn't fight the sun, it is too hot." Cottontail said, "If I had had moccasins and gloves, he would not burn me and I could have killed him!"

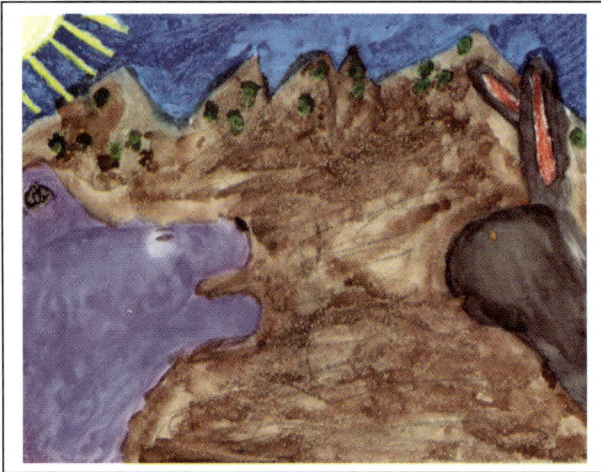

The Story of Cottontail
Brilee Forton

Folklore of the Stars

The state of the moon could predict the weather, and according to John Wesaw the following predictions could be made. A lying crescent meant stormy and cold weather whereas the opposite predicted precipitation. A crescent opening towards the west meant hot weather. But a crescent half-tilting in the opposite direction could mean half-bad weather, stormy and dry. If there was only a half moon on a Sunday then the bad weather could last for 1-3 days and be very cold or hot according to whether it was summer or winter. However if there was a full moon on a Sunday then the bad weather could last for two weeks. And finally if there was a ring round the moon then the bad weather could last for two months. Furthermore the Coyote stars (four of them) rise at 6 a.m. in the east. Their movements show winter, summer and springtime. The old timers used these signs to predict the weather. If all the stars were very bright it would be cold weather. The Indians call the Milky Way the Bear or the Seven Humans, and this is the center of the sky. There are two morning stars; the first one is called The Wicked Morning Star because it fooled people long ago when they discovered that there were two stars. The second one is the Great Morning Star or Evening Star.

The Rainbow's spirits show where there is gold buried under the earth. The Shoshone also call the Northern Lights the same.

How the Whales were Made or(Coyote's Large Catch)

Wolf and Coyote were sitting on the bank of a creek. Wolf said, "Now Brother, how shall we create food in the water?" Coyote replied, "We will make fish." "Show me how you will make fish?" asked the astounded Wolf. Coyote went down to the creek, grabbed some water in his cupped hand, and said, "Brother, this will be our food. Watch now." He poured the water into the creek and it turned into fish. "Now Wolf, you try it," he said. Wolf took a handful of water and then poured it back and it became bigger fish looking rather like salmon. Coyote said, "Now we'll let them grow for six or seven days, and then we'll return and see how they taste." They both fooled around in the country for some time and then they went back to the creek. They saw a large dam in the creek where they had left the fish –which was the work of the beaver. He was going to keep the fish for himself. Coyote said, "we don't like this, we created these fishes to go in the current here and don't like anybody to be a stingy man and hold it up. We'll take out that dam and let the fish go and tell the beaver not to do that any more." "If you want fish you can catch them like we do," he said to the beaver. They tore down the dam and let the fish out. All the fish headed west and grew big. They went towards the setting sun, into the ocean (they are the whales there). The people like to fish and they go out fishing.[4]

Astral Notes:

1. In this story the mountain sheep are called *túkuna*, "the meat."
2. The bats are a different kind of bird. They are called *hónowic* (from *hóno* – magic), "devil's bird," because they are something between a mouse and a bird.
3. John Trehero´s comment: "there was a power struggle between the bats, both gave instructions to each other." Concerning the etiology, John said that the fact that the sheep went up sky-high shows that they went up the mountain and that they became a star constellation.
4. *A:nzai* told this story.

Chapter 3

Coyote or Trickster Stories

According to John Trehero Coyote and Wolf both stood on their hind legs, although they were like animals. Coyote - *Sžapö* - was a kind of *puhagant* (supernatural power), but Wolf was less *puhagant*, he just had to do what *Sžapö* told him to do. Coyote and Wolf fished in Jackson country, in the Snake River.

The Story of Wolf and Coyote
Sady Cunningham

Coyote is the First Medicine Man

Wolf said, "Brother, what are we going to do about disease if it comes to our people?" "There is going to be a disease." Coyote said, "I will be the medicine man, and I will kill the disease." Then Wolf said, "We'll try it out Brother; we'll try out the worst sickness there is, the smallpox. How are you going to kill it?" Coyote said, "I will put a person over a fire and burn him. That's what I am going to do if they get sick." This is how Coyote turned out to be the first medicine man.

A Story about Wolf and Coyote

Wolf and Coyote went on a war party and they made enemies for themselves. "Well, brother," said Coyote, "we won't live happy this way without having a war." "Why do you want a war?" asked Wolf. "We would like to steal something from each other," said Coyote. "I don't like that," replied Wolf. "I don't like having bad feelings among the people." "No," said Coyote, "we must have enemies; then we will feel like men." Wolf gave in and said, "where shall we go to find enemies?" "We'll go to the next creek and find our enemies there," answered Coyote. "We haven't many arrows," said Wolf. So they spent the whole of the next day making arrows. The morning after that they left and carried big bags of arrows on their backs. they arrived at the creek where there was very tall brush. Wolf said: "Lie down here and don't peep out, just listen- If you peep they might kill me." Coyote lay down in a bush while Wolf went forward, let off a shot and stopped the enemy. Coyote said to himself, "I'm going to see what my brother is doing, if he is making a good job of it or not." When he looked out from the bush the enemy shot Wolf, pulled off his fur and began to go towards their camp singing. That evening they had a big dancing party, but Coyote was lying there crying. The enemy broke camp the next morning and started to move off. "Well," thought Coyote, "the only thing I can do is to get my brother's hide. Maybe I have a chance to bring it back." He went to the place where the enemy's camp had been. They had all moved off but he followed their tracks. He saw an old woman who was all alone walking along the track. She walked with a stick and had a large load on her back. Coyote caught up with her and asked: "Grandmother, where are you going?" The old woman answered, "I am following the camp." "What are they having such a big time about?" asked Coyote. "They killed the mighty wolf, and are having a good time about that," she replied. "Do you take part in these big dance parties?" asked Coyote. "Yes," said the old woman. "I do." "When that Wolf's hide comes to me I'm allowed to slam it on the ground." That made Coyote mad. "Who's that coming over there?" he asked. The old woman looked away and Coyote hit her on the head and killed her. He threw her on the ground and stamped on her, and shook her so that her legs fell off. He skinned her and dressed himself in her clothes, put her load on his back and went on, using her stick as well. He cleverly imitated her way of walking. At last he came to a little hill where the enemy had made camp. A couple of young girls said: "well, we have everything done now, let's go to our grandmother." They went up to where Coyote was sitting, but one of the girls became suspicious and said: "what makes your eyes so bright? They look like Coyote's eyes." "Don't accuse me of being a Coyote," said Coyote. "You girls say things to me that aren't right." The girls prepared a tipi for Coyote. "Oh girls," he said, "I am so tired, I think I'll lie down." The suspicious girl whispered: "Hey, I don't believe that it is grandmother." The other one got mad and said: "who else could it be? It's her skin. Don't talk that way. Poor lady, she is worn out, she has no horses." Coyote lay there and listened. "Well," said the girls, "let's have something to eat." They made supper. The camp announcer, *bellahú,* came out and said: "Everybody get ready for the big dance. We'll have a great time, because Wolf has been killed now." Coyote was mad when he heard that. Everyone got ready and went out to the place where the dance was going to be held. Coyote saw the wolf skin hanging on a pole just like the buffalo head was hung in the Sun Dance. They started to dance and passed the pole counter-clockwise, one after the other. Each one said something nasty about the wolf, for example, "I'm so glad that he was killed." The last of the dancers was Coyote. He caught hold of the wolf skin, slipped it under his arms and at the same time pulled off the old woman's skin, threw it down and called out: "Hey, take this old lady's hide and dance if you want!" He then jumped away from the place holding the wolf skin. The people started crying. "I said it was wrong, I saw it was Coyote," said one of the two girls. Coyote ran to the mountain, looked for the skinless body of his brother, slipped the skin over the body, and started tickling the Wolf under his arms and under his feet. Wolf came to life! "Brother, let's go home," said Coyote. "We've got to have war once in a while!"

How Coyote got Buffalo Meat

Little Coyote had a white bobtailed horse. Wolf said, "Our people are starving now, what are we going to do for them?" "Well (*haígena*)," said Coyote, "the best way that I can think of is to get out and scout around and see where the buffalo are." "Yes," replied Wolf, "let's do that because people need food right now, they are only living on roots and berries and we need meat. Make an announcement in the camp and tell them what we are going to do so that they will know." Coyote jumped up onto his horse and announced: "We have to move camp tomorrow so that we can get some meat. I'm going out early in the morning to find out where the buffalo are." Early next morning, before daybreak, Coyote went over to his horse and said to Wolf: "Now Wolf, go in this direction, towards the north, so that I can meet you when I come back from my trip." He left and everybody packed up and moved along. Coyote found out where there were a lot of buffalo. When he met up with Wolf he said, "there's a creek over here, between us and the buffaloes, and we'll camp there tonight." They moved along and made camp at the little creek. Wolf told Coyote to announce what to do in the morning, and Coyote jumped up onto his horse and said to the people: "All you men, get your best horses and hold them ready by daylight. We are here now to get some meat. There are a lot of buffaloes on the plain here. Don't let the young girls go out there, but have the old women take their packhorses out there."[1] Coyote's wife was going to have a baby. Coyote said to his mother-in-law: "Bring three horses with you, and leave them up on the high bank so you can get on your own horse very early." They prepared themselves for hunting. Coyote rode at the front and announced, quickly and sharply, "let's go!" and everybody rode off. A great number of buffalo were killed. Coyote killed two, and so did Wolf. They packed the meat onto the horses and then returned to camp. Everybody had meat that night.

Story about Coyote and the Bobcat -šérokowic

Coyote was chasing around in the forest one day. He ate wild, red rose hips that were growing along the side of a creek. Soon he grew tired and said to himself: "I am going to take a nap," Then he went to sleep. Bobcat came along, and saw Coyote asleep under a tree. "I will have fun with Coyote," said Bobcat. He got hold of Coyote's ears, pulled them sharply and made them longer and more pointed. Then he grabbed Coyote's nose, pulled it sharply, and made it also longer and more pointed. Finally, he pulled Coyote's tail until it also became long. Sometime during the afternoon Coyote woke up and saw his shadow (higiá), became frightened and scampered away. He soon found out that it was his own shadow. "I have not had this shadow before," he said. "I wonder who has been fooling with me? I had no long ears, no sharp nose, and no long tail. I will go back to where I slept and find out who has done it." He returned to the place, looked around and saw some tracks and said: "Oh, it's Bobcat who fooled me. Well, I will look him up now and see if I can catch him when he is napping." Coyote followed Bobcat's tracks, and finally found him sleeping under a rock. Coyote cut off his tail so that it was shortened, balled his feet to make them rounder, made his ears pointed, his head round, and his eyes very big. Then he ran away. When it was time for Bobcat to drink, he woke up and went down to the lake. He leaned down over the water to drink, but drew his head up again when he saw something come towards him in the water. He jumped backwards and said: "what is that? It seems to jump when I do. It seems to be me!" Slowly he went to the water and made some movements, and the shadow did the same. "Oh, I see," he said, "Coyote did these things to me, since I did the same to him." Bobcat tried to change his appearance, tried to make his tail longer, pinched his feet, pulled his ears back, tried to change the form of his head, and screw up his eyes, but everything he did hurt. "Well," said Bobcat. "This is how I will look from now on. We played tricks on each other, so that's alright." In this way Bobcat got a short tail, round feet, pointed ears, round head and large eyes, and Coyote got long ears, a pointed nose, and a long tail. That's the way the animals treated themselves way back, when they could talk – in nïmïrika's time.

The Story of Coyote and the Rolling Rock

Old man Coyote used to wander alone. Someone said to him "In the middle of the desert there is a big, black rock, a medicine rock. Whenever you pass there, don't leave it unless you have given it something, a moccasin or an arrow, for that rock has a wonderful *puha* (medicine)."

Coyote wandered along the old trail and said to himself: "I want to see that rock, just to see what he will do to me. There is no use in giving it anything, it is nothing but a rock." He ran up to the rock and said to himself: "I'll just piss on it to see what it is going to do." He raised his back leg and dirtied the rock. He saw masses of things on the top of the rock – bows, arrows, moccasins – they were gifts that people had put there, people who believed in the power of the rock. But Coyote said: "It is just a rock; I don't believe it has medicine." Coyote went on his way and after a while looked back. It looked as if the rock was moving. "What's that now?" said Coyote. "It can't be so, it's just my imagination – *nánaxi:a,* that makes it look as if it is moving." He went on walking, but the rock rolled after him quicker and quicker. "Well," said Coyote, "I have lived in this world for a long time, but this is the first time I have seen a rock rolling like that. However, I am too fast for it." The rock rolled up the hill where Coyote was and came very close to him. "I have never seen a rock running up a hill, they only roll down," said Coyote. He jumped onto a side trail, but the rock was still after him. "Oh," said Coyote, "the rock is right behind me! Well, I don't think he can cross that river there, it is too wide, and its bottom is too rocky, he will get caught there." Coyote jumped down into the river and swam over but even the rock – *timpi,* went over, it jumped over the stones in the river. "Well," said Coyote, "he will stop in the middle of the river, and if not, the river bank will hold him up." But the rock also went up the riverbank! Coyote looked around and saw a snake sitting there. "Hey, Snake," he said, "the big rock is chasing me." – "Well," said the snake, "I can't do anything about that." – "Maybe you can kill him with your poison," said Coyote. "The rock will get me if I get tired, so I will keep going." Now the rock came on and rolled over the snake, killing it. A buffalo was grazing up among the hills. "Hey, Uncle Buffalo," said Coyote, "can you help me with this rock that is chasing me?" – "I'll try it," said Buffalo. "You have done something dirty to this medicine rock. You shouldn't have done that. But I will try and help you." Buffalo sank his head, and stood all prepared to meet the rock. The rock increased its speed, ran right into Buffalo, hit his skull, and killed him.

Coyote then met a falcon – *gïni,* which had youngsters. Coyote said, "Sister can you help me out?" "In what way?" asked the falcon. "I don't know," said Coyote, "I am tired now. That big rock is chasing me." The falcon said: "You have done something dirty to him. Get behind me, maybe I can do something." She flew high up in the air, and then dived straight toward the rock. "Pooh," she said, and hit the large rock with her wings so that it went to pieces. "Well, brother," said the falcon, "you could have done it if you had known it." "I am pretty tired tonight sister," he said. "Well," said the falcon, "don't play that trick on a medicine rock any more." "I will never do it again," said Coyote. "I will go down by the river and clean myself up."

He went down to the river and there was a bear that was digging for roots. "What should I say to this bear," said Coyote to himself. "He doesn't look so good. Well, first thing I shall say will be, Hey, Bear, you have got big feet," and then he fell down on his stomach laughing. "What other things can I say?" he asked himself. "Well, I'll say: 'Hey Bear, you are a kind of plugnose, you have got small nostrils!" After that he threw himself once more on the ground and laughed. But the bear didn't care about that, he even laughed himself. "What's the next thing to say to him?" ´ Then he shouted: "Hey, Bear, you have got a short tail!" Once again Coyote fell down on his stomach and laughed. "What else can I say to him?" "Shall I say: 'Hey, Bear, you have got short, stubby ears! Coyote shouted out loudly: "Hey, Bear, you have got stubby ears!" Once more Coyote fell to the ground laughing. "What more can I say?" he thought. "Hey, Bear, you have got small eyes," shouted Coyote. But now the bear was tired of him. "This Coyote is teasing me all the time," he said. "I will do what the rock did to him. I will chase him until he has got his tail dirty." Coyote was lying on the ground laughing and thinking what he could say next to the bear. But suddenly the bear came rushing towards him; Coyote jumped up and started to run. Coyote did his best, and ran around a rock. As the bear passed him Coyote hit him on his tailbone. Now the bear was scared and shuffled away with Coyote running after him. After a while Coyote broke off the hunt. "Well, I am tired," he said to himself, "I'll quit right here." He went down to the river and washed himself. "Well," he said, "I am going to stay right here overnight, and I will never again do rude things and say bad words to the rocks."

The War of the Birds [2]

Here is the story about the birds going to kill a huge monster.

(*Pandzó:aβits)* Crow blacked himself all over, so that he looked as he does today. And two little sagechicken brothers - *tïa ižapö* had grey blankets, as they have today. Coyote said, "Well, we want to know who is a good sneak (assassin)." Those two sagechicken brothers wanted to be scouts, so one of them said: "Just let me and my brother try, we'll come down that hill there, see if you can find us." They went up the hill and came down sneaking through the sagebrush. Coyote asked the birds, "Can you see those two brothers over there?" "Yes," the birds answered. "Well," said Coyote, they don't make good scouts, let's try a rattlesnake."

 The rattlesnake crawled down the hill. "Can you see that rattlesnake coming over there?" Coyote asked. "No," the birds replied. "It's too hard to see him. "Well, he is the man we want then," said Coyote. "Keep the two brothers and try them on something else." These two chicken brothers could throw a *wŭnza?* - a type of club.[3]

Coyote took a piece of hide and threw it, and the sagechickens made a good hit. First one brother hit it, then the other brother also did the same thing. "Well," said Coyote, "we'll bring you boys when we come down in a cooley, so you can kill that mother of yours." The sagechicken mother was actually a monster - *nïmïrika* and a (2-headed antelope) was acting as a guard. "Well, I guess we are all set now, let's go," said Coyote. "First we'll make an imitation of antelopes." He made the birds look like antelopes, and dressed them in antelope hides. These antelopes now came down from the hills, and went to the creek to drink. They got pretty close to the buck antelope that was spying for *nïmïrika,* the monster. The snake got close to the buck antelope, and when he made a jump, the snake bit him between the toes; for Coyote had told the snake, "that's where his heart is, you can kill him quickest there."

The birds shouted, "Snake has killed the two-headed antelope!" Coyote took the antelope hides off the birds, and they all went to the cooley. "Well," said Coyote to the sagechickens in a low voice, "here's the place where you have to do your shooting. We'll all wait and watch." Soon they heard the cackling of the old sagechicken. The youngest sagechicken said, "mother has already seen us." "Well, hurry up!" said Coyote. The oldest sagechicken rushed up and killed the old hen with his wŭnza? Nïmïrika fell down and acted dead.

Eagle was up in the air, he said: " Nïmïrika is lying there by the fire taking a nap." So Coyote said, "That's where I and Raven are going now. When you boys see us shooting, run over there." Coyote and Raven ran and started shooting. Coyote knew that nïmïrika's soft spots were under the arms, so he told it, "throw your arms up!" " Nïmïrika did so, and was filled up with arrows under his arms, and was killed. They left Nïmïrika there with its back towards the fire, and they went home singing.

A Story about a Man with Buffalo *Puha* - supernatural power

It is said that years ago a man, a buffalo *puhagant*, collected all the buffalo skulls on the ground and put them in rows. He sang a song to the buffaloes, asking them to get up. And then the buffaloes got up, and there were ten times as many buffaloes as there were before. He said, "go up on the hill we want a hunt tomorrow." Next morning he said to Coyote, "tell the people not to take the legs, heads, and hides of the buffaloes we are going to hunt." Coyote told the people, "just cut up the meat, but leave the bones, feet, and heads there. Then they can get up and go again, so we will have another steak later on!" They did that.

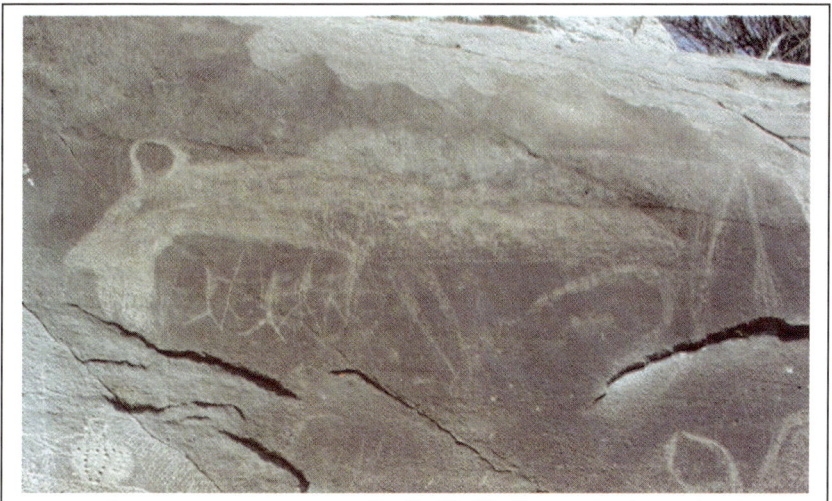

Coyote and the Sun Dance

One summer's day Coyote was up in the mountains hunting. He stopped just before sunset. He heard a noise from a drum and someone said, "Boys, you have danced all day now. We will sing once more, and then let you boys rest." Coyote heard this but couldn't see any people. He looked down at the meadow in the middle of the wood where the voices seemed to come from. He said to himself, "I can't see anything; where are they dancing? They could be on the other side of the hill. Well, I will hurry up! They said that there was only going to be one more song." He ran into the wood, went around the outskirts of the meadow and once again heard a voice say, "Let's sing another song, a long one, and then rest." Coyote said to himself, "It sounds as if it is coming from over there, at the other side of the meadow." He wandered across the meadow and came upon an old elk skull; inside it

29

the mice were holding a Sun Dance. He listened once more, yes; it was in there. He said, "Hey, boys, let me in, so I can help you sing." "No, you are too big, you can't come in," replied the mice. Coyote said, "Oh, there must be some way. Let me in so I can help you." "We can't let you in," they said, "and this is our last song." "Yes," he said, "and I must sing it with you." "No, we can't help you come in here," they said. "What about if I come in where the head joins the neck," said Coyote; "there is a big hole there, maybe I can put my mouth in there and sing for you." He stuck his head in, but got it caught in the skull, and when they stopped dancing he couldn't get his head out of it. The mice said, "Well, that's all of it, we quit the Sun Dance," and they wandered off. Coyote had to wander away with the skull on his head and he went down to the river. He saw some people who were camping on the other side. "Well," he said, "I know, maybe those boys can take off the skull." He went down into the water and started to swim over the river. There were some boys playing by the river and when they saw him they shouted, "there's an elk swimming across here." The men in the camp hurried to fetch their bows and made their way to the beach. They saw the elk head, fired off some arrows, and killed Coyote. Then they pulled him out of the water and lay him on the shore. "Oh," they said, "this is Coyote, look what happened when he got his head stuck in the elk's skull!"[4]

The Death of Coyote

Wolf and Coyote were anxious about what was going to happen to them. Wolf said: "Take a couple of men and go to Feather's Hill and scout around." Coyote took two men with him and said to them: "Now boys, we have to be pretty careful about our scouting here." "Why?" they asked, "there is nobody here." They followed the path. Two Indians who were out scouting around saw Coyote coming along the path, and hid themselves in the sagebrush. "Hey," said one of them, "you take notice what they look like when they come out on that hill." Coyote and his friends climbed up the hill. "See those Coyotes," said one of the Indians. "Yes, I see them," answered the other one. "Think that they are Coyotes?" "Well, I will look again." The Coyotes carried on along the path. "No," said the second scout, "they are too low in front, and their feet are too big. Those are enemies." They crept along carefully as they went down the hill and ran to two other Indians. "Hey," they said, "Let's kill those guys. Half of us go ahead, half of us stay here. Let them pass the first two of us, and we'll take them between us." Coyote and his two men now went past the place where they were waiting. Then they called out to their friends who were ahead, and they shot the Coyotes. They found that one of them was Old Coyote, and he had a bow and arrow under his skin.

Coyote and the Round Dance

One evening Coyote jumped up onto his horse and rode around the large camp announcing, "We will have a round dance tonight. There is a bad disease coming from the east, and we will have a round dance to protect ourselves. When we come to the place where the fire is, I will tell you what to do. Everybody get something to eat right away and hurry up there. This has to be done right now." All the animals gathered together where he had told them to, and he positioned himself at the front and said, "We dance with our eyes closed every time I lead off a song."

Coyote sang, "*gakawuwun, gakawuwun,*" meaning "the packrats are making trouble," (if anyone happened to have their eyes open). They danced with shut eyes, and Coyote stepped back to the back of the ring and said, "I will stand guard, to watch for that sickness." He stood close to a fat buck deer, took out a knife and stabbed the deer in the heart. Then he started to dance again. "Oh," he called, "there goes one fellow – stop! Now you see: this man did not believe what I told him, he looked and sickness came into him. Well, we have to go and bury him among the rocks." Coyote made sure that no one else was hurt, "just one man got hurt this time." They carried the dead deer to the rocks and buried him there. Later Coyote went there, took up the dead deer and carried him to his family, so that they had a good meal.

"Coyote, you have to call for another dance," said his wife. Now Coyote's brother-in-law, Magpie came in, and said, "Say, brother-in-law, what makes my little nephews so fat? I see some bones out here; you must have had some pretty good food." Coyote answered, "The packrats took the bones here somehow, and the kids have played with them." "No," said Magpie, "if that is so the bones would not be as greasy as they are, you must have killed somebody." Coyote's wife gave Magpie a piece of fat and said, "take it home and give your family some food." Magpie took it in his mouth and flew home. When he and his family had eaten the fat he said, "Well, I have some suspicions about my brother-in-law. I think I will go over to Bull elk's tipi to find out if he knows anything." He flew over to Bull elk's tipi. "Bull elk," he said, "I have come to get a little information! There are things I want to learn. Something is not right here." "Well, said Bull elk, "we were talking about that , too." "What do you think of my brother-in-law's ways?" asked Magpie. "Well," said Bull elk, "it looks as if Coyote calls together these gatherings to kill somebody, in order to get something to eat." "Wait now Bull elk," said Magpie, "let's have it this way: we'll get a couple of kids who do not look very good, so that Coyote does not want to eat them.

Mountain sheep kids don't look good when they are small; they are thin and have big heads and big bellies. Coyote doesn't look for that kind of stuff, be wants big, fat animals. We will ask those two mountain sheep kids to half-close their eyes when they dance so that they can spy and see who is doing the damage in the next dance." Coyote called for another dance gathering. "If we don't dance that sickness will clean us out," he said. The animals gathered together again. Everyone came from the mountain and the desert, they made a fire, and the two small mountain lambs arrived to watch Coyote. Coyote started the dance; "*gakawuwun, gakawuwun,*" he sang. The animals closed their eyes and danced around. Coyote killed another buck deer, but then the mountain lambs shouted out: "Coyote stabbed him!" "Hey boys," said Coyote "you were not supposed to have your eyes open!" But the mountain lambs shouted: "we saw you stab him!" Coyote ran away and everyone else ran after him, but he managed to hide himself. They picked up the dead buck deer and carried him up the mountain and buried him.

After a while Coyote came forward and took the body home with him, and the family ate it up. Then Magpie flew in. "Brother-in-law," he said, "is it right what the kids said?" "No," said Coyote, "Bull elk made a bad plan against me. I made this dance to save you folks from the sickness, but I don't want to make it any more." Then Magpie said: "you did it just to get something to eat. You better give me some fat for that." Magpie was given some fat and flew off. All the other animals ran away from Coyote and refused to share camp with him. They said to him: "You are a serious disease yourself!"

Coyote Becomes Blind

Coyote went down the hill. "I am hungry," he said to himself. "I just can't struggle hard enough to keep myself alive. I am half-starved all the time. There must be something that keeps me from getting something to eat. I always have bad luck. But sometimes I hit it pretty good. Well, I will go over there to the river bend and take a nap. Maybe I will have a good dream." He lay down by the bend in the river on a little pile of driftwood. Then a voice called. "Coyote!" He awoke from his slumber and said, "I wonder whose voice that was; it spoiled my dream. I dreamt about a big piece of fat, and I was just going to eat it when this voice woke me up." "Coyote, you had better take a big bite out of me," said a piece of fat that was drifting in the current and was pushed up to the surface by the water and landed just by the pile of driftwood. It was Coyote's dream that had come to life. "Hm," said Coyote, and took a large bite out of the piece of fat. Then he said to the fat, "there are some more coyotes at the next bend of the river, and they too are hungry, so you had better float down there to let the next coyote have a bite." The fat floated on. Coyote licked his mouth clean, and cleaned his teeth from all the small slithers of fat. Then he rushed through the brushwood and lay himself down at the next bend in the river, pretending to be asleep. Soon the piece of fat came floating to the surface and said: "Coyote, take a big bite out of me and you will feel better!" Coyote took a big bite and said to the piece of fat: "there is another Coyote at the next bend and he is pretty hungry, you have to feed him too!" The fat floated off. Coyote let out a satisfied sigh. "Ah…!" he said, "I want another bite!" This time though he forgot to wash himself, and rushed away to the next bend in the river and lay down pretending to sleep. The fat came along and said: "Coyote, take a big bite out of me!" But then he saw the remains of fat that hung from Coyote's teeth. "Well," commented the fat, "he looks just like the Coyote who took a bite out of me a while ago!" So the piece of fat jumped back into the water.

"Well," said Coyote, "that's what I always do; I always make mistakes, I always spoil it for myself. But next time I will be careful. I guess I'll go up along the creek. I really feel pretty good. That hillside up there looks good to me; I will take another nap there." There was a small creek just below the hill where he was standing and he saw some children go there and start playing. They shouted to him: "come down, come down!" Coyote listened and said to himself, "I wonder what those kids are doing; I must find out if it is something good." He went down the hill to the children. "Hey, kids," he said, "what are you doing?" They replied, "We throw one of our eyes up in the brush and then a big carrot comes down together with the eye. That's the way we eat carrots." "Hey, wait, let me try that," said Coyote, "I am finding it difficult to get something to eat." "Well," said the children, "you have to try it, then let us see if you get any carrots." "What do you say when you throw your eye up?" asked Coyote. "We say: my eye, my eye, come down from the brush. Instead of the eye we get the eye and a carrot. You better try it!" "I will try it," said Coyote. "What kind of brush should it be?" "There are two kinds," said the children, "be sure that you throw your eye on the right kind." "What if I make a mistake?" "Then you lose your eye." They showed him the right kind of bush. Coyote took out one of his eyes, threw it on the bush and said "*Púipai, púipai, púipai, púipai,* - my eye, come down." Then came a large carrot together with his eye. "Oh," said Coyote, "I learnt a good trick now; thank you boys!" Then he wandered off further down the creek. "Well," he said, "I want another carrot." He took out an eye, threw it at a bush and said "*Púipai, púipai, púipai, púipai,*" and the eye came back with a large carrot. "Well," he said, "I will walk on and now and then get another carrot." But he threw one of his eyes at the wrong bush without thinking, and he lost it. "Well," he said "if I take the other one it will come down." He threw the other one but it didn't come back and he was blind now. He carried on walking along the creek when he heard someone say: "Look out, look out!" "It sounds as if they are having an arrow game over there," said Coyote to himself. "I will listen and then go in the direction where I hear the voice coming from. He carried on and came closer to the players, who were calling: "Look out, look out!" Wolf was among them.

"Hey, younger brother," said Wolf, "come over here, you used to be good at the arrow game. I have lost lots of games, but I would not have done that if you had been here." Coyote had covered his eyes with a piece of cloth, and said: "the wind is blowing hard and sand has got in my eyes, and I have to carry this piece of skin so that I can see a little bit." Coyote joined in the game. "What is this," said Wolf. "He is usually good at this game but now he throws the arrows in every direction! Pretty sure we will loose this game." When they had finished the game and lost, Wolf said: "Let's go up to the camp and get something to eat." They made their way to Wolf's tipi. Coyote was given a large portion of food. "Well, elder brother," he said to Wolf, "I want to sleep." Wolf said, "Move back a little bit and lie down on that buffalo robe and have a rest so you will do better tomorrow at the arrow game."

When Coyote was asleep, Wolf went over to him, lifted the eye covering, and saw that Coyote had no eyes. Wolf called to his wife and said: "Come out, I want to tell you something." They went out of the tipi. "My younger brother has no eyes," said Wolf. "I wonder what has happened to him, and I wonder how he manages to get along. You watch him here, while I go up in the mountains. I will kill a mountain sheep, take its eyes out, and then put them on my brother." Wolf left and went up the mountain. Soon he had killed a mountain sheep, and then he took out its eyes and made his way

34

back to camp. Coyote was still sleeping so Wolf put in the mountain sheep's eyes. When Coyote woke up later on he found that he could see. "My eyes bothered me," he said, "but I can see pretty good now. We can play another game in the morning." The next morning they arranged another arrow game and this time they won. Coyote said, "Brother Wolf, I can't play any more games now. I have promised to visit Skunk." "Listen here now Coyote," said Wolf; "I want you to quit running around with those sort of people. You only make tricky work, and you and Skunk are both the same. You always get the worst out of it." "Oh," said Coyote, "I promise not to do that any more. But I promised Skunk that I would go there." "All right, go then," said Wolf. Coyote left and went to visit Skunk. That was the last time for a long time that Wolf saw his younger brother.

Skunk Tries to Kill the Coast-Dwellers
(The following story about Coyote and Skunk is a direct sequel to the above story.)

Coyote said, "Brother Skunk wants me to visit him, he wants to talk plans with me." Wolf said, "You have to let me know what your plans are, so I can understand them." Coyote went to Skunk's tipi. "Hello," he said, "Brother Wolf wants us to report our plans to him, so I have to go back and tell him." – "My plans are to smoke out all the people that live on the coast," said the

Skunk. "They are sending disease into our country. But I will kill them. That way we could live better." – "No, that is no good," said the Coyote, "I know that Brother Wolf won't like it. If you spray your *Tú: paganap* - black fog all around us there will be no people left. I don't like it." – "That makes no difference," said the Skunk, "I am going to do it anyhow." "Well," said Coyote, "wait and let me tell my brother what your plans are." "All right, go ahead," said the Skunk, "I will send my wind-medicine - - to Wolf when he comes, and then I will send out my black fog, and you will get it too." The Coyote went to the Wolf's camp and told Wolf what Skunk's plans were. "Well," said Wolf, "I'll tell you how we will get rid of that stuff that Skunk is bragging about." In their camp they had a mouse with a white stomach, - *Tošapambonai*. He was sent with a message to go to Wolf's tent. Wolf said to *Tošapambonai*: "Do you know how Skunk keeps his stuff? You have been in every camp, so you should know." - "Yes," said the mouse, "I know where he keeps his things." – "Well, where does he keep his black fog?" – The mouse answered, "I guess I know where he puts it at night when he takes it off. He generally hangs it up on the second pole from the door in his tipi," "Well, *Tošapambonai*," said Wolf, "you go down there and take it and bring it up here. Do that for your own protection and for the protection of all of us."- "If that is the case," said the mouse, "I will go down there and get it." "But don't touch the bag, just cut the string off," said Wolf. The mouse went down to Skunk's camp, and cut off the string without touching the bag, just as Wolf had said, and carried it to Wolf's camp, where they burned it. The next day Skunk sent out his wind *puha* signal, to wait for Wolf at the pass. When Wolf arrived he gave the wind *puha* signal and Skunk came out. He tried to send out his smell towards Wolf, but he couldn't and he went back into the tent. "I have lost my black fog," he said to himself. "I wonder who took it away?" He smelt all around. "Oh, that little rat, he took my scent!" Wolf came and said: "We have got your stuff, and we will keep it away from you so you do not hurt more people. The things you told Coyote were not good."

Coyote and the Wild Geese

Coyote walked along the creek. "Who is that making all that noise up here on the creek? he wondered, and looked up and listened. "A-ai, a-ai, a-ai," said the geese. "Hey, my nephews, what if I go with you?" said Coyote. "Why?" asked the geese. "I want to look the country over with you birds," said Coyote. The geese collected around him, and said, "If you keep your mouth shut and halloo when we halloo, it will be alright. We will give you some feathers. Where do you want to fly with us?" Coyote answered: "I want to fly at the tail end of the V. There's a guy I like to see, and I want to halloo like he does." The geese gave him some feathers and stuck them onto his arms, and said: "We only halloo at certain times. When we halloo once

36

all of us say a-ai." They flew up into the air. Over every lake they passed they hallooed, but Coyote said: "wo, wo, wo." The leader of the geese said: "Coyote you are not hallooing right. You should halloo like we geese do. Next time you halloo like that we will take your feathers out." But the next time they flew over a lake Coyote again said: "wo, wo, wa!" Then they plucked the feathers off him so that he fell into the lake. There were some minks standing on the shore and they said to each other: "say, it looks like something was dropped over there. What could it be? We better go over and save him from drowning." They dived into the lake. When they got close to Coyote they asked: "Hey, what are you doing in the water?" "It's me, nephews," said Coyote, "can you take me to the shore?" "Well," they said, "yes, we can." Then they took him to the shore and said, "We will call you Coyote [i.e. fool] from now on, and we will be called (minks that eat fish)."

Coyote and Menstruation

Coyote created everything.[5] He said, "We must arrange it so that women folk have blood every month. Now, my daughters you are going to have menstruation – *hú:nöywa.*" He threw blood on them. "Hey, girls, you are *hú:nöywa* now, you have to be in a menstruation tipi - *-húnagan* now and can't come out until after four days. That's the way all the women folk are going to be." To the men he said, "if you fool around with *húnagan*, you are going to be very ill - *máušunt.* You can't kill anything. You are going to throw up blood and die with haemorrhages."

The Marriage of Eagle's Daughters

One evening Eagle asked Coyote to make an announcement for him:[6] "I am going to put my two daughters up in a tall pine tree. The one that can knock them off the tree will marry them; it does not matter whether he is old or not." That night it was pretty noisy in camp, as everyone knew that the daughters were beautiful, and the camp dwellers discussed who was the best shot among them. Early next morning the men gathered at the tree and tried out their luck one after the other. Each one was allowed two shots. The first to shoot was Coyote, but he shot over and under, and the others had similar luck so that no one managed to hit them. Everyone had used up their two shots except a little boy who had a bow and arrow. Coyote said to him, "Hey, why don't you try? If you make it, you will have the young woman and I will get the older girl." But everyone said: "No, Coyote, you can't make your own rules now; we have to live up to Eagle's rules." Coyote said to the little boy: "Try, friend! Lift your leg up when you shoot, you might hit something." The boy took aim and shot off an arrow, and he nearly knocked them off. "Try it again brother," said Coyote, "try it again!" The second arrow knocked the girls out of the tree and Coyote said, "Oh, my brother, he got the girls!" The others said "No, Coyote, you can't tell him what to do, and take one wife away from him; the girls belong to the little boy." Coyote said: "Brother, don't listen to these people. You should give me one of the girls, since I helped you to get them." Eagle said: "No, I made the rule that whoever could shoot them off the tree would have them. They belong to you, little boy. And you girls, pack up your things and go with the little boy to his grandmother's place where he lives. And don't fool around with Raven or Coyote; don't listen to them, but just stay with the little boy."

They went off to the little boy's grandmother, who was bringing him up, and they stayed there. But the oldest girl only stayed one night. The little boy – *Násituhĭpö?*-(the boy who wets his bed, from - nási- piss on himself and – *tuhĭpö?*-(*ŭpö* – boy) slept with the girls that night, but wet the oldest girl's dress. So the next morning she ran away. She married Raven, who was a chief on the other side of the river. He had also tried to shoot down the girls in the tree.7 The younger sister stayed with the boy though. She said: "My sister asked me last night to go with her but I refused, for I don't want to break Father's rules." After breakfast the young boy played with his toys. The Grandmother said to the younger sister "Go down to the river bank and fetch the wood that I have piled up there. There is my rope and also my blanket." "Yes," said the girl, and went down to the riverbank and piled the wood onto her back and made her way back to the camp.

Meanwhile the young boy had tied up his feet with some rope and put the rope over the poles in the roof of the tipi. "Grandmother," he said, "cover up your head and turn the other way, and don't watch me. When I get through I will call on you." Then the boy pulled on the piece of rope that was hanging down and in that way pulled himself feet first up to the roof of the tipi. He stretched himself and pulled himself down so that he took on the stature of a man. Afterward he called his grandmother and she saw that he was now a good-looking man. She said: "Grandson, you look good, you are tall and slim. Your wife won't know you; we have to tell her." They put up another tipi and the woman returned with the wood and put it in front of the tipi. She looked up and stared and stared. The grandmother said "Come in young woman, this is our camp." The girl went in and saw a good-looking man lying on the bed. Grandmother said, "Don't be afraid, that's your husband, *Násituhĭpö?*."

In the evening the girl went out to bring some wood. When she went in again she said, "They are announcing across the river that the scouts have seen lots of buffalo in the desert." *Násituhĭpö?* said, "The announcer will be around pretty soon and tell us." Coyote came across the river and said, "They have seen a lot of buffalo in the desert. You boys, get your horses ready early in the morning." *Násituhĭpö?* tied up his horses, and got out his bow, arrows, knife and rope. His wife asked what kind of horses she could ride. He answered: "Take the pinto horse to ride on, lead the two black ones. I will lead the smallest black horse and ride on the bay."

Now Coyote came a second time and announced: "All you women, have water with you for your husbands. They get dry when they are riding fast." Before dawn the next morning they were all sitting ready on their horses. They rode up the hill and stopped there. Coyote said: "Hold on boys, hold your horses so we can all ride together. We will all get some meat, don't rush and spoil the hunting."

The people looked at *Násituhĭpö*?; one said, "I wonder who this young man is?" Eagle's younger daughter (who is with him) was supposed to get married to *Násiduhĭpö*? But that is not him, that is another man. And the oldest girl married Raven, so the girls didn't obey Eagle's rules." "No," said someone else, "*Násituhĭpö*? is a powerful man and he can change himself in any way he wants. I know that that horse belongs to him and it is fast; I'll bet that he will kill a buffalo before anyone else does." The sun had almost risen by now. "Well," said Coyote, "we can't wait any longer. I guess we are all here so let's turn loose. Go ahead boys and kill the buffaloes!" They rushed forward and the young man on the black horse killed a buffalo before anyone else did.

The Antelope Hunter who Guessed the Riddle and Got the Girl

This is the story of *Tia?kant* – antelope horns owner (*ti* – got, *a?* – horn, and *kant* – owner). He belonged to a tribe living in Nevada and California, and he was called *póhogsnituhipö* – sagebrush houseboy.

Tia?kant went out every day with the hide of an antelope's head, and packed arrows on his chest. He killed lots of antelopes and his mother made lots of buckskin suits for him. They had quite a lot of antelope meat. But he was not a very good horseman; he was a sagebrush house boy. But still he carried on hunting.

One day when he was hunting he saw that a big camp had moved in by the creek. From the mountains he watched the people in the camp for a while. On his way home he met a man on horseback coming from the camp. The fellow said, "where have you been *Tia?kant?*" "I have been out here in the desert killing antelopes, and I am just going home now," he replied. "Are you single?" asked the man. "Yes, I am a single man." "Say, the chief is putting up a prize for the one who is a good guesser: the man who guesses correctly will marry his daughter and she is a good-looking girl." Don't you want to go down there *Tia?kant?* You might make the right guess." "Yes," said *Tia?kant,* "I will try it, It seems like a good chance to get a woman." *Tia?kant* went home and said to his mother and father, "I think I will make a trip tomorrow to the new camp that is over the mountains. I want to visit the people there." He did not say what he was going to do there.

The next morning he took his antelope hide and his antelope head and his arrows. His father said, "Son, why do you take those things with you if you are just going to pay a visit?" The son said, "Well, I can't go without my stuff. I have to have it with me all the time." "Alright son, we will see you when you return." The boy left and went through the desert. Soon he heard a voice in the sagebrush calling, "where are you going *Tia?kant?*" "I am going to visit the new camp over there to see what the people are going to do." "May I go with you, maybe I can help you?" said the voice. It was *Tošabamporai* – Mouse. "Alright," said *Tia?kant;* just jump onto my pack, you can ride up there." The mouse jumped up onto the pack.

They came to a slough creek. *Tia?kant* heard a voice again and it said, "Hey, *Tia?kant,* where are you going?" "I am going to pay a visit to the new camp over there," *Tia?kant* replied. "Can I go with you?" the voice asked. "I might be of some help to you. "Alright, I will take you along." That was Mink – *Pǎsawi,* and he jumped up to the place where Mouse was. As they went along Mouse said to Mink, "I wonder what *Tia?kant* is going to do?" But *Tia?kant* heard them talking and said, "I am going to visit the big camp.

40

I want to see some people there." After a while he saw something hanging on a tree with spider web all over it. The thing asked, " *Tïa?kant* where are you going?" "I am going to the camp over there, I want to visit the people and see what they are doing," said *Tïa?kant*. "Let me go with you," said the voice, "I might be able to help you." "Alright, I will take you along." That was *Ïpɛ? – sleep-maker,* the butterfly.[8] Mouse said to *Tïa?kant,* "you have to pick him up, since he can't walk." He put the butterfly on his pack and went on over the mountains.

They came to a little creek close to the big camp, and they camped there. *Tïa?kant* saw a lot of men sitting around in a circle, and in the middle of the circle the chief was asking every other man, "what is this hide made of?" Whoever was able to guess correctly what kind of fur it was, would win the chief's daughter. It didn't matter whether he was young or old. "What kind of fur is it?" said the chief. "It must be mink," said one man. "No, you missed it," said the chief. *Tïa?kant* was on the end. "What kind of fur is this?" said the chief. *Tïa?kant* said, "it must be young mink," but he also missed it. "Well," said the chief "everyone can come back tomorrow morning and we will try it again."

Tïa?kant went to his pets. "Say, *Tïa?kant,"* said Mouse, "I wonder if this is a good chance to run down to the Chief's tent and listen to what they are saying there?" "Yes," *Tïa?gant* replied, "you and Mink go there and take Butterfly with you. You can find out something; maybe they are talking about the hide now." The pets went down to the big camp; Mouse went inside the chief's tipi, Mink and Butterfly stayed outside. Mouse sat down behind the bed, and listened. The chief said, "Daughter, don't think that these guys will be able to guess what this hide is because it's a strange fur that nobody ever thinks about. It isn't an animal fur. This is a black lice's fur." And then Mouse heard the story of this particular fur: One day when the chief's daughter was combing her hair a louse fell out. She called to her mother, "Hey, mother what's this? It is the first time that I have seen such things in my hair." "That's a louse – *Pú:šia,"* said her mother. "We'll ask your father about it and see what he is going to do with it." The father came in and the mother said, "our daughter has found a bug in her hair, and wonders what you are going to do with it." The chief said, "Daughter, you tie that bug up in your sleeve so it will keep alive. We will see how big it will get." It grew and grew, it got bigger and bigger, and when it got to be a good sized animal, the chief killed it and made a fur out of it.[9]

After Mouse had heard all this, he sneaked out of the tipi and all the three pets went back to *Tïa?kant*. "Say, *Tïa?kant* we sure found out what kind of fur it is." "What is it then?" "It is the fur of a louse." "A louse's fur, how could that be?" said *Tïa?kant*. "Well, that's what the girl's father said. Be

41

sure to get up early and take a seat before they start tomorrow,[10] so you can make that hit." "Oh," said *Tïa?kant,* "that's good. I will say *púšiambï?gida* – I guess that it is a louse's fur."

In the morning Coyote went around the camp announcing, "Come on boys, let's have that guessing game again today. Everybody should gather here in a circle." The men formed a circle, and *Tïa?kant* sat in the first quarter of the circle. The chief asked the first man, "What kind of hide is it?" "I think that it's a mountain lion," said the first man. "No," said the chief, "you missed it." The next man said, "It must be a muskrat," but that was wrong. Again, the next one said, "It must be a mink." But that was also wrong.

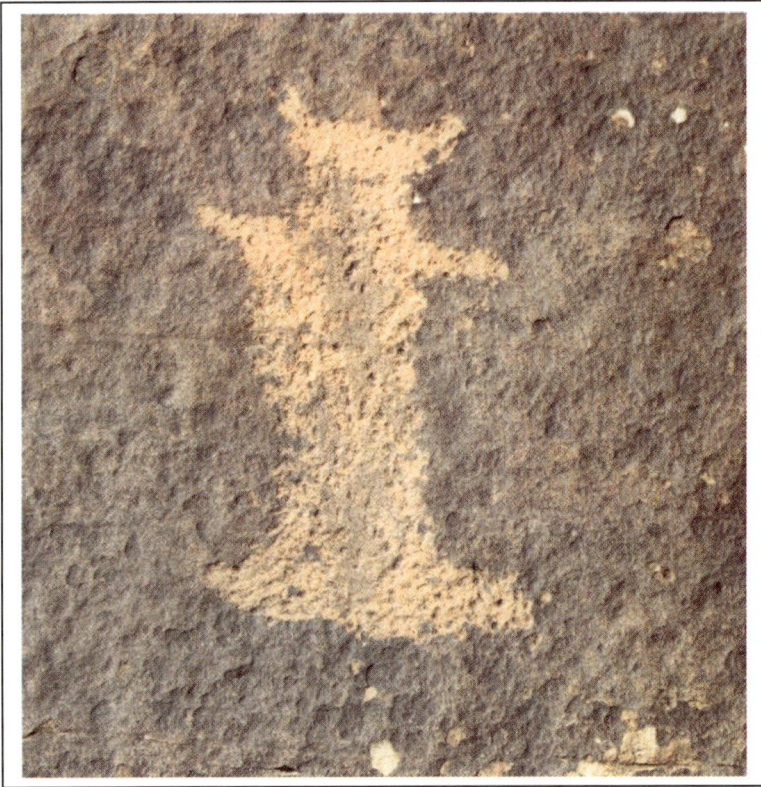

Finally, it was *Tïa?kant's* turn. "What kind of fur is it?" asked the chief. *Tïa?kant* said, "*púšiambï?gida.*" The chief said *"uš, uš, uš."* And Coyote announced, *"Tïa?kant* made the right guess, he wins the girl." The chief said *"Tïa?kant,* over there is my tipi and your woman is in there. I will take you over. Take this fur with you so she will know that you are the man who guessed what kind of fur it is." The chief took *Tïa?kant* over to the tipi, and introduced him to his daughter. "Oh, father," she said, "I was just wishing

42

for this kind of man: he is always hunting and I won't go hungry. This man hunts all the time, that's why they call him *Tïa?kant.* I have heard about this young man."

The chief said, "wait, we'll just hear what Coyote is announcing." Coyote said to the men, "why didn't you make the right guess? It was a simple thing. Now that big-bellied *Tïa?kant* took the woman away from us." *Tïa?kant* stayed for a while with his father-in -law and went every day over to feed his pets. His wife asked him, "Why do you always go to that tent, why don't you bring it here?" But he said, "No, that's taboo - *má:ušiun* - I can't bring it here."

One day *Tïa?kant* said, "We will go to my place. My father and mother are alone and I am worried about them." They started out, but first went over to the tipi. He took his stuff and his pets. His wife wondered why he should take them along. "These are my good friends," he explained. "Maybe they told you something, and that's the reason that you guessed correctly." "No, you are wrong. I don't use them for such things; they are my friends." They went on and came to the tree where *Tïa?kant* had got the Butterfly. He said *Ïpɛ,* I will leave you here now, thank you for having come with me." When they came to the slough, he left Mink. "Mink," he said, "there are plenty of fish here; you could live here. Thank you for having come with me." They went on, and *Tïa?kant* stopped again. "Well, Mouse, there's a lot of seed you could live on here, so I will leave you here where you were before. Thank you for having come with me."

Tïa?kant's mother happened to be tanning hides outside when they arrived. She said to the old man, "it looks like our boy is coming home and he has someone with him." "Let me see," said the old man, "Oh, our son has got himself a woman, isn't that great? *Tïa?kant's* – dear wife - *nanasuigaint."* The mother said, "Girl, take some of that buckskin and make yourself a new dress or two if you want to." And the girl did, and also made some moccasins for herself.

The young couple had a nice tipi and plenty to eat. They lived there for just over a year. After a while they had a little boy. The little boy grew up and learned to walk. *Tïa?kant's* wife said, "let's go and visit my mother and father now, I want to show them our little boy." *Tïa?kant's* mother and father brought some meat and said, "take as much meat as you can pack." *Tïa?kant's* mother had tanned some hides, and said to her son, "take these to your wife's mother and father, they might need them."
 Tïa?kant and his wife packed their things and went away. They walked with their packs on their backs and travelled all day. Late in the afternoon they arrived at the chief's camp. "Oh, somebody is coming over there," said the

chief's wife. "It looks like two grown-ups and a little one." The chief said, "Our daughter must have had a child." His wife said, "That's our daughter coming home and it must be her child walking by her side. I am going out and meet them; I am so anxious to see the little one." She went out to meet her daughter and said: "this must be my little grandson!" A young man who was pitching arrows close to the chief's tent said, "Oh, it's *Tïa?kant* coming! That big-bellied thing made a child for that young woman!"

There are many stories about how Coyote makes plans with different animals, and they are put in a special order: deer, owl, beaver, yellowtail, moose and elk. Here is yellowtail.

Coyote and the Yellowtails

Coyote arrived at the camp of his brother-in-law, Yellowtail bird – *yuwazít?*[11] *Yuwazít?* said, "brother-in-law, I have not much to eat, but you must eat something with us." *Yuwazít?* went out with his spreadkiller – *winzá,* and called to the yellowtail birds: "*W ĭdodiž, w ĭdodiž, w ĭdodiž!*" When the birds flew in he killed five or six of them, and prepared them for Coyote, who ate them up. "Brother-in-law," said Coyote when he had finished his meal, "you better come down and visit me tomorrow so we can make plans, and see what the other men are thinking." The next morning Yuwazít? went over to visit Coyote. "Brother-in-law," said Coyote, "we will have a good talk here. I will go round to the camp to see what our plans should be." They talked, and talked, and talked. At last Coyote said, "you can have something to eat before you go back home." So Coyote went behind his tipi and called, "*W ĭdodiž, w ĭdodiž, w ĭdodiž!*" The brown coyote birds – *ïžapöhújudui*[12] -flew in and collected round Coyote, who threw his *winzá?,* at them and killed five or six. He cooked them and gave them to Yuwazít?, but since these birds did not taste as good as the *w ĭdodiž* birds Yuwazít? said: "No, brother-in-law I don't want them, I have had a good breakfast this morning. Give them to my nephews, they are hungry, they will eat them." Now Coyote did just what Yuwazít? had done earlier, he took away all the feathers and threw them into the brushwood and they all flew off.

Coyote said to his wife, "Well wife, I think that I will go over to see my brother-in-law, Moose, to see what he thinks." "You better not invite him to come over here because we are so poor," said his wife. "Oh, I can manage it," said Coyote. The next morning he went over to Moose. When he was nearly there the dogs started barking and one of the children shouted, "Mother, somebody is coming." "Who is it?" she asked. "I don't know who it is," said the boy. Then she said to her husband, "Somebody is coming." "Look out and see who it is," said the man. "It looks like Coyote," she said.

44

"Oh," said Moose, "I know why he is coming." He is collecting ideas from each of us. Now you boys sit up and keep quiet."

Coyote entered. "Hallo, brother-in-law, I came over to see how this plan sounds to you. I want to hear what you say about it." Moose said, "Whatever plans they make, it's alright with me." "Well," said Coyote, "if it is that way with you, then the majority will rule." They talked and talked. At last Moose said, "you better have something to eat before you go." Moose went out of the tipi and cut out a piece of his muzzle just under the skin. He grilled it over the fire: Oh! It tasted very good! "Well," said Coyote, when he had eaten, "if you decide anything, come over in the morning and let me know." Moose came round next morning. The children called to their mother, "somebody is coming." Coyote's wife said, "It looks like your Uncle Moose. You boys sit up now and be quiet, for Uncle Moose is here on important business." Moose entered. "Well, brother-in-law," he said to Coyote, "I will go with the majority." They talked and talked and then Coyote said: "Well, brother-in-law, it is a short day and I don't want you to leave before you have had something to eat." Coyote went out and cut off a big piece of his muzzle. He took it in and asked his wife to cook it before his brother-in-law went home. "Brother-in-law," said Moose, "I really don't feel like eating anything as I had such a big breakfast this morning. Give it to my nephews. I know that they will eat it." And Moose went home.
"I have to visit my brother-in-law, *Kyúp* –elk,"[13] said Coyote. "I have to see what he thinks about it." The next morning he went over to Elk's tent. The dogs barked and one of the children who was playing ran over to his mother and said, "Mother, someone is coming." The mother looked out and said, "It looks like your Uncle Coyote. I'll tell your father about it." "Oh," said Elk, "I have heard that he is going around hearing what folks think about the plans he is making."[14]

Coyote went in. "Hello," he said, "I want to know what you think about this." Elk said, "Whatever the others think, then that's all right by me; but we should get everyone together. What is the main question?" (He was the first one who asked.) "Well," said Coyote, "there are two different things that we should decide amongst ourselves: how we shall live, and where we shall live. Some say, we shall live in the water, some say, we shall live in the mountains, and others say, we shall live in the desert; but most of my brothers-in-law want to live in the mountains."

"It is alright for me to go with the mountain people," said Elk. "I like to live up where it is high all the time. Brother-in-law, you better have something to eat before you go." Elk went out and cut out a big piece of his steak; his wife cooked it and gave it to Coyote. When Coyote had eaten he said, "Come down tomorrow brother-in-law, you might want to think a little." The next morning Elk said to himself. "Coyote is crooked, and he might be fooling around with us; he is too foxy. He has been known to double-cross us."

Coyote waited for Elk to arrive. His wife said, "Why do you want to invite all these men? They are not as poor as we are, and here you want them to come over to our place. Still you don't treat them right." "Well," said Coyote, "I want to see what they think."[15] Then Elk arrived, the dogs barked and the children rushed in and said, "Somebody is coming!" "Oh," said their mother, "that is somebody your father invited. I suppose it is Uncle *Kyúp;* you boys be quiet now so that we can hear every word your Uncle says. Some day we might call on you to witness what he said. Listen closely!"

Elk entered. "Hello," said Coyote, "here is a seat for you." "Well, brother-in-law," said Elk, "all of us deer, mountain sheep, moose, and myself, are going to live in the mountains." "That plan is good," said Coyote, "that's a very good plan. And beaver will stay in the water, and yellowtail, he only comes once in the spring - from the south, that's a good plan. I don't blame him; it is too cold here in the winter. Buffalo and Antelope haven't given me their plans, they don't like me. They say, 'go away, Coyote, you lie too much. Owl has got no plans at all, and I am by myself. I will live on rabbits and such stuff." "Now, Coyote," said Elk, "you must have some reason for having me come here."[16] "Well, brother-in-law," said Coyote, "I want you to have supper before you go, it's getting late." He went out and cut off a large piece of his steak and his wife cooked it over the fire. But Elk said, "Oh, I don't really feel like eating just now, I had a big breakfast this morning. Just feed that to my nephews. Now, brother-in-law, I think that is how it is going to be from this time onwards."

Skunk Tries to Destroy Wolf's Camp

One evening Skunk arrived at Bobcat's camp. He sat down on a rock and told Bobcat stories. Bobcat became sleepy, but he placed a reddish, rotten piece of wood next to him. When Bobcat had fallen asleep Skunk took out his bow and arrows and shot at Bobcat, at least that is what he thought. However, when the dawn came in the morning he saw that he had shot at the piece of wood instead of Bobcat.

"He was the first to fool me," said Skunk, and walked off. He walked towards the camp of Wolf. But Bobcat lay hidden alongside the path and heard Skunk mutter to himself: "There is no one greater than me in the world. If the animals run after me they will be dead before they get close to me. If the floodwater comes, it will stop flowing before it can even reach me, nothing can hurt me! I will clean out Wolf's camp. I will arrange it so that Wolf will call the people together and I can put a cloud on them."

Bobcat heard all this. Skunk went on, "there is only one thing that I am afraid of! When anybody whistles it makes me scared. Nothing else can scare me. If they see me coming they will be paralysed, so I can pick up anything I want to eat." Suddenly Skunk started to whistle, and made himself jump. "If anybody whistles like that," he said, "it means danger to me." Again he whistled and jumped. "Hmm," he said, "I am afraid of that, it makes me nervous!" Once more he whistled and jumped again!

Bobcat had listened to everything that Skunk had said and ran off ahead of Skunk to Wolf's camp. "Skunk is coming," said Wolf. "What does he want here?" asked both Wolf and Coyote. "I don't know but I guess that he wants you to call for a round-dance." "No," said Coyote, "Skunk is dangerous." "Yes, he is dangerous," said Bobcat. "I think that he wanted to kill me last night, but I got away. He was telling me stories to put me to sleep, and he tried to shoot me, but I put a piece of rotten wood alongside where I was lying. Pretty soon he shot at it with his arrow, and thought that he had killed me; but in the morning he knew I fooled him. Today I waited for him to come on the trail, and I overheard everything he said. "What did he say?" asked Coyote. "He said that he wanted Wolf to call all the people together so that he could put a cloud on you and kill you." "We will fix that fellow," said Wolf. "How will we do it?" asked Coyote. "Somehow," said Wolf; "somebody will knock him out, and we will cut out his scent." Just then Skunk arrived and went into Wolf's tent and he fell asleep. Wolf and Coyote jumped on him. Wolf took a sharp knife and cut out Skunk's "black fog."- *Tú:paganap* - That is why you can nowadays smell that stuff, but it is not dangerous like it was in the old days.

The Story of the Pine Nuts (*pignon*)

All the birds and animals, everyone from the desert, were going up to have a handgame with all the animals and the birds from the mountains. They all painted themselves: Raven blacked himself all over, Magpie put on a white shirt and white wings, the Woodpecker dressed up, and all the others did the same. Coyote and Wolf were the announcers, and they had arranged the meeting. Coyote said, "Now people, we are going to play a handgame with the people in the mountains. We are going to beat them to win the pine nuts tonight, for we need them. We have no pine nuts on the prairies.

If we don't win the pine nuts we will steal them. The bear, elk, squirrels and all the other mountain animals don't need the big ones; they could have the small nuts; but we need the big ones (*that Coyote!*) I want everybody to do his best now so that we can get them. Rabbit, you get your flute; and you two Woodpeckers, you have long bills. Be ready. If our people don't get those nuts with the first game, then Rabbit, you play your flute so that the two old ladies who are charge of the pine nuts that are tied to the lodge-poles will go to sleep. Then, Woodpeckers, you break open the bag that they are kept in, grab what you can, and take the seeds to make them grow here."

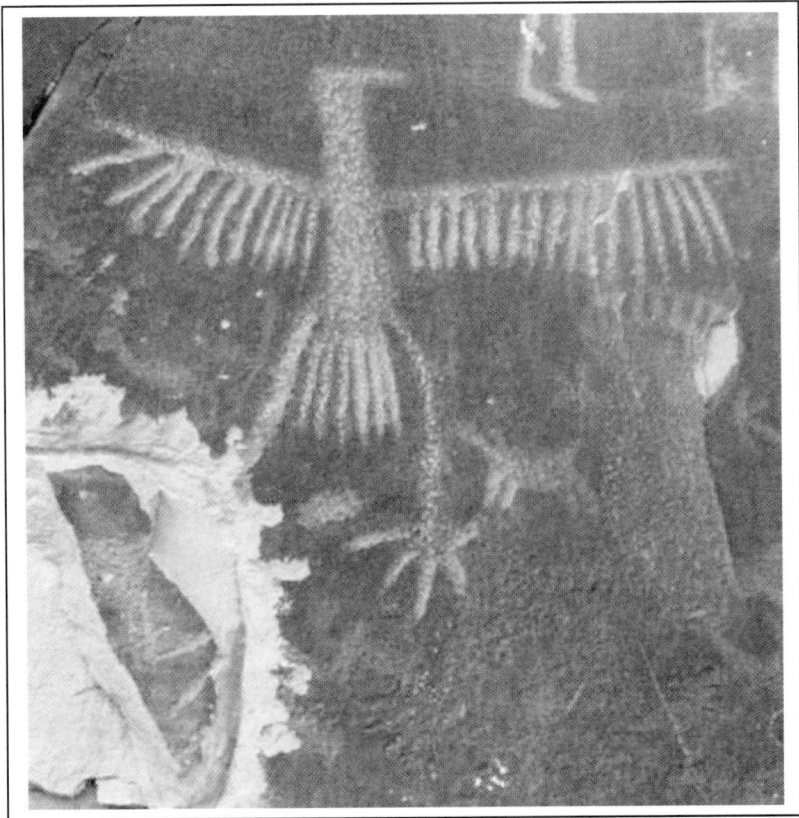

They all went to the meeting with the mountain animals; they played the handgame with them but did not win the pine nuts in the first game. Coyote whispered to Rabbit and the two Woodpeckers, "Hey, those fellows won't win the big pine nuts so Rabbit you go and play your flute, and you Woodpeckers go do your job." Rabbit went down to the ladies' camp, and played and played and played his flute non-stop. The old ladies went to sleep. The Woodpeckers sneaked into the ladies' tipi, put their bills into the bag with the big pine nuts and broke it, so that the pine nuts fell out. The Woodpeckers put them in a bag that they had brought with them and went up to the high mountains and gave the bag to the Sandhill Crane and Raven. Raven had of course painted himself black so as not to be visible to his enemies. Crane and Raven, who were the swiftest among the desert birds, ran away with the bag to the West. The two old ladies woke up the next

48

morning and one of them said, "Hey, friend, something happened to us. That stinking Rabbit came in here, got to the pine nut bag and tore out the bottom, then he stole all the pine nuts!" "Well," said the other lady, "we will have to notify the announcers that we were put to sleep by the Rabbit and that the Woodpeckers stole our pine nuts. Come on, let's go."

In the meantime Coyote said to the slowest of the desert people, the toads, frogs, turtles and other animals: "You better start running, for there is going to be a big fight here." But the Wood tick said, "I am the slowest one, I might not get anything; just give me one pine nut!" "No," said Coyote, "you can't have any, you just get away now with the others!" "No," replied the Wood tick, "I don't run fast, they will kill me first, so let me have one." "No," said Coyote again, and the slow animals went away.

Now the two old ladies arrived. They told the Mountain squirrel, who was the announcer of the mountain people, what had happened. The Mountain squirrel said to all the mountain people, "We heard from the two old ladies down there that two long bills stole our nuts from where we had put them, so now we have no nuts for breakfast." Elk, the boss of the mountains said, "All we have to do is to go chase the thieves and catch them."

Wolf, Coyote, Antelope and the other desert people ran away, and the mountain people started running after them but Crane and Raven were by this time far ahead. Elk said, "We have to get those nuts back! Porcupine, shoot some quills into their feet so they can't run so fast." Elk also started running. After a while the mountain people had knocked out Wolf, Coyote, and all the other fast desert animals and they saw Crane and Raven running ahead.

Elk said, "Raven has the bag under his wings --now he hands it over to Crane. – Now Crane hands it back to Raven. Moose, kick them over!" Moose knocked Crane down, and then caught up with Raven. But Raven had the seeds under his leg feathers and when he was knocked down his leg broke off, and they kicked the leg over in a sand-draw. Elk said, "Well, we'll take a rest now, and then take that bag of nuts home with us."

They rested a while. Then Elk said, "Well, let's take that bag home now. We have whipped them all." But they couldn't find the bag! Moose said, "When I kicked Raven I saw something fall over there into that sand-draw." "Well," said Elk, "we better look over there." They tracked one leg running up the sand hill to the woods. They saw fires along the ridge of timber. Elk said, "We can't do anything; they are cooking the pine nuts now." The mountain people lost their pine nuts and the pine eaters took them to Nevada. That is why the big nuts grow down in Nevada.

Notes on Coyote Chapter:
1. John Trehero made a comment that young girls should be left in the camp, "they can't pack the meat like the old ladies; meat is too heavy for young girls."
2. John Trehero said that this was a true story.
3. This club has eight sharp points, a sort of tomahawk that is used to kill sagechickens. It is sharp edges of flint and a hardwood handle.
4. John Trehero replied here to my comment that Coyote had also been killed in another story. "They killed him, but maybe he came to again, for he was a wonderful man."
5. This was said in a slightly ironical way.
6. John Trehero said that Coyote had made this announcement to Wolf, Eagle and Raven.
7. In those days the animals could talk and each group of animals had their own chief. However, Wolf was also the chief over the Coyotes, not Coyote himself, for he was the announcer. Still, Wolf always asked Coyote about things because he "was smarter."
8. The butterfly has got this name because when it was a pupa "it was a boy."
9. This story was told last. John was unsure about where to place it; it could be first, last or in the middle as I have placed it.
10. The exact wording was: "Sit up early when they start."
11. *Yuwazit*[?] = "full fat bird." The yellowtail birds are called *w ǐdodiž,* i.e. "plenty" (*w ǐdo*) "fat" *diž*).
12. *Šžapöhújudui* = "Coyote's game birds" (perhaps sparrows?).
13. *Kyúp* is Coyote's word for elk.
14. John's comment was: "he didn't tell what his plans were, he only went around to get something to eat!"
15. John commented here: "Coyote had no plans, he stole all of them."
16. John's comment here was: "Coyote couldn't answer this question, and he abruptly changed the subject to **food!**"

Chapter 4
Stories about Some Remarkable People and Animals

Yellow Wrist and the Moccasins

A little boy was crying for something to eat. Yellow Wrist took off his moccasins, buried them in the ashes of a fire, and said: "We'll have something to eat pretty soon." After an hour or so he dug up his moccasins, and, instead of moccasins, he took out two buffalo tongues.

Yellow Wrist and the Goose Eggs

Another time there was nothing to eat. Yellow Wrist told everybody to go outside for a while. He put a pot on the fire, covered it with a buffalo robe, and prayed for two dozen goose eggs. Then he said, "Well, folks, come on in, we'll have breakfast now." His folks and family came in. He told his wife to lift up the buffalo robe. There were twenty-four goose eggs in the pot!

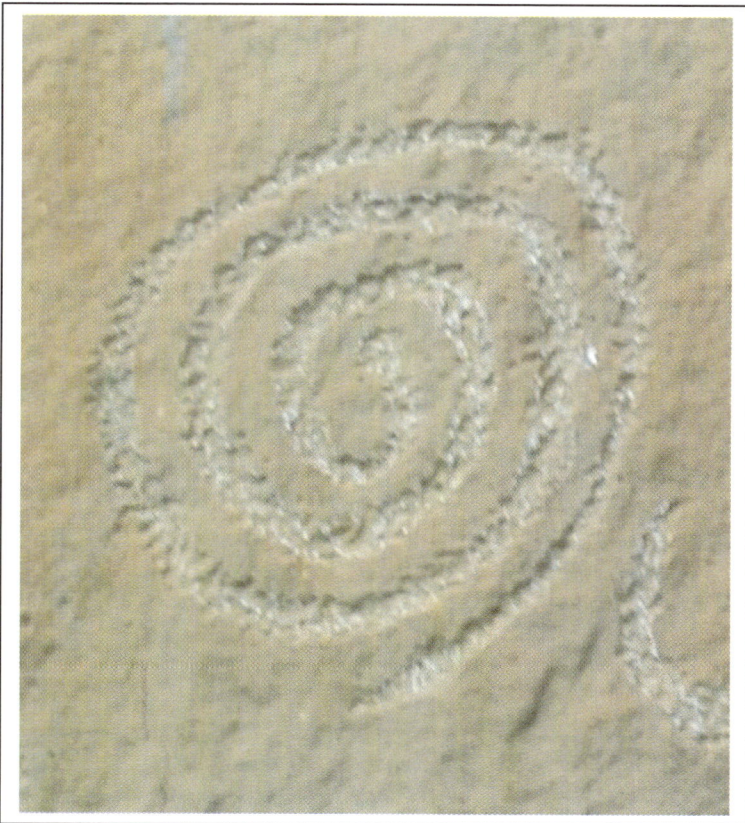

How John Trehero became a Medicine Man

John said that both the white doctor and the Indian medicine man "make the same good job." This is John's own tale as to how he became a medicine man:

"When I was a boy around fourteen years old I took the horses that we had west of the mountains to my mother over on the East Side of the mountains. I took them over the mountains and arrived in the evening at the highest part of the North Fork of Popoagie[1]. There are rock drawings at that place and I had a dream there. I didn't mean to go to sleep there." John went to sleep without knowing that there were rock drawings situated there. In his dream, "I got scared, it was like having a nightmare;" he wanted to wake up but he couldn't. "You can't when spirits come into the dream." In the dream, which took place "pretty near daylight," John saw an eagle and a bear – they looked like these animals, not like humans. They had no clothes, and didn't change form or shape.[2] "I woke up, saw the signs on the cliffs, amongst other things, a bear and a snake. Then I saddled up the horses and rode on." From this dream John obtained snake power, "can cure snake bites," and he therefore became a "snake medicine man," – *dogwapuhagan*.

In the same way John obtained bear power from that dream; that meant that he "could kill people with his bear power." So he also became a "bear medicine man," – *agwapuhagan*.

A year after this vision John obtained eagle power. It also happened in a dream one night. "The eagle, when I first got it, was right with me," he said. [The eagle said] 'Tomorrow by noon they will bring this boy (N.N.) to you; you must make him well, cure his pneumonia, and blow the sickness away.' "The next morning a little boy really was brought to me and I blew on him. Five days afterwards I saw him playing with some other boys. The father came and asked me how much he owed me? That's up to you," I said. "I don't charge for my job, but you can give me presents if you like." The father said, "It would give me great pleasure to do something for you. I don't have any money, but I would like to give you a horse."

John went on: "In my dream the eagle looked like an eagle. It talked to me and gave me instructions: it said how I should cure the sick, what I should do so that I shouldn't lose the power, and how to avoid danger. Many times since then I have had visions of both the eagle and other spirits – p*uha,*- power -I cannot mention them all. When I was young I had a lot of knowledge of medicine. I saw things coming at night, and the next morning what I had seen came true. I knew if someone came to me to be cured. I was a good curer – *puhagan* – when I was in my thirties; now that I am older, my powers are weaker.

John suggested that one evening, before the weather became too cold, I [Åke Hultkrantz] should accompany him to the Dinwoody rock drawings so that I could try and get some *puha*. I suggest that we take Tudy with us, but John remarked that in the Sun Dance Lodge during the summer Tudy had said that he was afraid of rock drawings' *puha*, but John didn't know why[3]. John said that we could sleep in my car a little way away from the rock drawings, not too close to them because "you might get scared. The spirit will come to us through the radio mast, and then we can see it in our dreams," he says. In the presence of Deborah (John's wife), John explained the ritual that we should observe at our destination before we tucked ourselves into our blankets. First we should get into the water naked and at least splash a little water over the top part of our bodies; then we should paint a little red on our chest and forehead; then smoke. Finally, we should devote ourselves to what is called *púhawido?* – sleep at Medicine Rock.

Concerning women and puha; John saids that if a woman cannot be cured by a puhagant then she should go to the rock drawing to be cured. At Dinwoody she should sleep out on the rocks by the tree. Puha will come in her dream and say that she will be cured. Women can also be púhagant, and he went on, "my mother was a mighty púhagant; she just touched the sick person once with her hand, and he was cured.

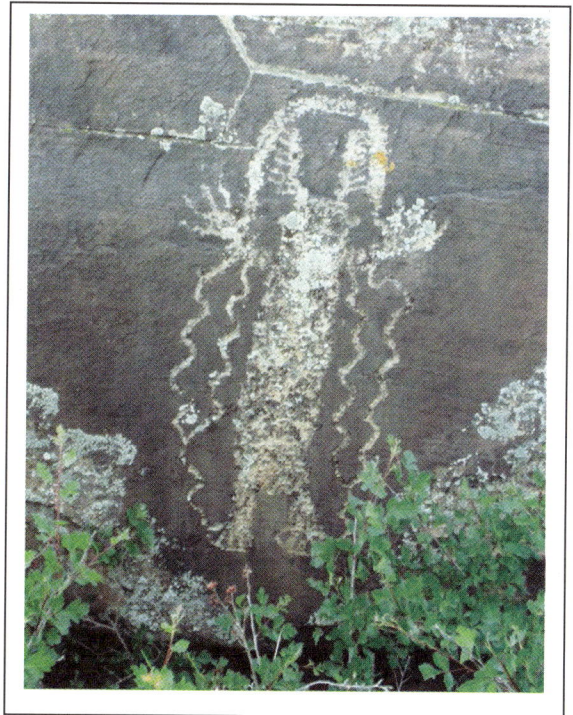

53

John Trehero and his Vision of Thunder

John has had several visions of thunder – *tóywoyaget* – "the rain-clouds are crying." He saw a spirit enshrouded in something; "it looked like steam but it was fog." The thunder spirit itself is described as a "sharp-nosed bird, little as a thumb, looking like a humming bird, but faster." The message of the thunder is: "*Puha* told me not to eat stuff turned over with a knife or sharp stick. So I don't want a knife used in cooking: it might come back on me; I might have bad luck for three to four months. Therefore I am afraid to eat in restaurants."

"When you hear the thunderbird coming in the dream, it will tell you the news and what is going to happen." Both in 1917 and in 1941 the thunderbird that looked like a humming bird told John that there was going to be a war. "In my dream he [the thunderbird] let me look into a blue mirror and I saw dead soldiers lying side by side."

John had visions of both thunder and lightening in his dreams, when there was actually thunder and lightening going on in the sky outside. Every summer, starting in April, John had dreams about thunder; he had them "up on the mountains, towards sunset." During the winter he never dreamt about thunder. "He [the thunder], is quick. Sometimes you just hear his voice, you don't see him. He talks fast, too. Some places you will miss his talking."

John also had visions of lightening – *eygagú?ce?.* "A person who comes into contact early in the spring with lightening, gets an electric shock. Lightening you see as a fire, not as a being; but you can hear him talk." John made a comparison with the radio: "it is driven by electricity; you hear voices, but you don't see anybody." John described his first vision of lightening: "I have seen, *eygagú?ce?.* it was in a dream. I saw a blue streak of light in the north, it curved like this"- here John demonstrated with his hand the zigzag of the stroke of lightening. "It said, *Parokogare,* you make smoke early in the morning, and I'll tell you what to do later in the summer season."

The lightening said that during the night while John was asleep. In the morning John asked his mother, "what it meant," and she said, "Take water and rub it on your arms then make smoke." John did as he was told, and then said, "If I hadn't done so, it would have been no good to me. Later on in the summer *eygagú?ce?.* told me to go into the Sun Dance lodge and pray together with the others for the sick boys. That's all he told me that summer. Later on he gave me power to cure people."

John's Dreams That Came True

Two nights ago I dreamt that I stood in front of my house just before dawn. Two men came towards me and said: "See here *Parokogare* there is going to be trouble in the east; there is going to be a terrible war." I looked toward the house and then back again and then I saw two eagles sitting on the fence [the rodeo fence]. Sure enough I woke at sunrise and I prayed, "Almighty God, don't let it happen again [meaning that a war should break out]." Here Åke H. asked John if he had had any idea that Egypt and Palestine were on the brink of war, and John replied that he had no knowledge whatsoever of any presumptive war!

A year ago I, [John], was alone in my house, but in my dream two beavers appeared. They said, *Parokagare,* your grandson gets into Seattle today." In the morning I got up and told *Puyep* that I had dreamt of what I had wished for during a long time. "What is it?" she asked. Johnny was in Seattle yesterday, I said. And two days afterwards he was here. "You never made a miss yet," said John's second wife, *Puyep.* "What you see in your dreams always comes true. You see it two or three days before it happens." *(They married in 1917, she was the widow of Tome Ute).*

I took part in a Sun Dance at the Crow Agency in 1945. My friend, Old Coyote, led the dance. "Hey," he said. "I want to know when is this war [World War Two] going to quit that we are in?" 'Well,' I said, 'we don't know, but I am working hard to find out when.' "Well, when you have a dream, tell me," said Old Coyote. That particular night was the second night of the Sun Dance, and just before daybreak two bears came to me. Later on the next morning Old Coyote asked, "Got any news yet?" 'Yes,' I said, 'but you must keep it to yourself. The war is going to quit right away.' (That was at the end of August, 1945). "Well, I want to have this announced at 10 o'clock," said Old Coyote. 'No,' I said, 'you have to wait and keep it secret, announce it tomorrow.' "Why tomorrow?" he asked. 'I might be able to find out a little bit more,' I replied. We danced all that day, and the night fell. 'Now I will dance till 12 o'clock,' I said. When I went to bed at midnight I said: 'Don't bother me, leave me alone.' I didn't wake up until three in the morning. Then I told Old Coyote: 'the war is over now. We'll get the news sometime today.' At the morning ceremony Old Coyote and his assistant came up to me to get some fresh air. 'Now you can make that announcement,' I said. He called the announcer, *Taizeni,* who was an old man, and he announced that World War Two was quitting now! Nobody believed what he had said. At dinnertime the superintendent, Bob Yellow Tail came over and went round the camp singing "World War II ended yesterday!" The people asked *Taizeni* where he had got his news. He replied, "They told me to announce it." 'But where did they get that news,' they asked. "In the Sun Dance Hall. They kept it quiet for two days until they were sure today.' The Crows came over and shook our hands!"

In November 1945 I was down at the Crow Reservation again. I had been invited to attend Thanksgiving. One Crow, Joe Wallace, had not come home from the War with the other Crows. His mother and wife were very unhappy about this, but still they had had no word from him and he had been very frequent in writing home. They asked me to help them. "John," they said. "We are so anxious, we wonder if he is alive or not."

The following Saturday evening there was a meeting and many people attended. It was a medicine meeting, with all the Crow medicine men. Each one of them had tried to find out where Joe was. I was the last medicine man to try. There was a mirror, and I painted half of it black and the other half white. "Now," I said. "We'll pick out two men to watch this glass, and see if they can see anybody in the black space." We started singing, and a little light turned up on the white side of the mirror, went over to the black side and went over to its rim. I stopped the singers. The light stayed where it was.

I asked them, "Do you see that light?" 'Yes,' they said. "That's Joe," I said. "He is here in America, here in the U.S.A. Maybe his folks will hear from him tomorrow." Next day Joe wired from Cheyenne, Wyoming that he lacked money. They sent money to him, and the day afterwards he arrived by train. Joe shook hands with me and said, "You are a great man."

Some Examples of How John Cured Sickness

Right after the Sun Dance this year a girl came over to me and said, "The white doctors have told me that they have to take away my appendix [i.e. that she had appendicitis]. John, I want to find out from you before I go under an operation if you can help me to get better without an operation." I told her to sit down and I examined her. 'No,' I said, 'I don't think that you need an operation, you have no appendix. You have to vomit the sickness out.' I took out one of my feathers, worked on her for ten minutes, and then she threw up stuff that looked like yellow leaves. 'Well,' I said, 'just go to the doctor and let him see you again.'

The next morning she visited the doctor and in the evening she came back to me. "John," she said. "You are a very wonderful man. That doctor looked into me and said that it [the appendix] wasn't there anymore. Now I want to pay you the sum that the operation would have cost me. The white man said that it would cost $600." 'No,' I said, 'my medicine doesn't tell me to take money.' "Well," she said, "the way that I feel about it is that I'll give you something tomorrow." 'Well,' I said. 'Let's first see if this works, let's see if you are not sick for three weeks.' "What food should I eat?" she asked. 'That's up to you; all food is good for you.' "I'm satisfied with what you say," she replied. After three weeks she came back and said: "I haven't felt any pain these last three weeks." Then she gave me some blankets and money, and said, "I want to give you these presents, I feel good over this."

Some time ago, in 1943, I was at the Crow Agency. When I was going to eat breakfast somebody came along, his name was Dick. He said, "I want you to help straighten out my brother. He is crazy: he has no clothes on, he has not eaten for three days and he is playing with sticks, throwing them in the air like kids do, although he is fifty years old." I kept studying the crazy man, and then all at once I heard in my ear a thunder-like noise. 'Oh,' I said to myself, 'now I know what it is; they [the spirits] want me over there where the crazy man is.'

I went there and saw the man; he had only a collar on, and a sock on one foot. No other piece of clothing, and he was walking around playing with the sticks. Together with Dick and another man I went up close to him and stopped. Then I blew three puffs from a cigarette towards him. He stopped and looked around. I blew three more puffs. 'Hey, Rainbow!' He said, "Is that you?" He walked towards me. The other two fellows were afraid, but I stood there, and he came right up to me and shook my hands. "Friend," he said, "I am glad that you found me." I shook hands with him. 'Dick,' I said, 'Give me his clothes and we'll put them on him.' But when he got the clothes he put them on himself. I said: 'Give him smoke.'
 Lots of people were watching. Then he said, "as soon as I smelt that smoke, the craziness went out of me. It was as if my brain was in a sack, and I felt that this sack broke in the middle and [the craziness] went out of my head." Dick wanted to pay me for my help, but I told him that I didn't want any money. However, he said, "When you are ready to go home, I'll pay your fare." He did just that. .[4]

I, [Åke Hultkrantz], mentioned to John that I had a bad pain in my cheek (it was an infection in the left part of my mouth). John raised his right hand, and almost touched my cheek, while staring at it with a very determined gaze of energy. Then slowly he sank his hand onto my cheek, kept it there some few seconds, and then quickly took it away. A really amazing show of psychic power!

This is how John cured a patient that another medicine man could not [as told by John]. Once Morgan Moon gave up a boy. He said that his *suáp* – spirit, had gone. But the boy's father came to me and said, `John, I hate to loose my little boy, and you are the last one I turn to. If you do good to my little boy, I will give you a fine present.` "It's up to you Frank," I said, and I went over to see the boy and to see what I could do for him. His heart was still beating. "No," I said, "Morgan could have saved this boy; his *suáp* hasn't gone yet. If it had gone then his heart would have stopped beating. That boy was choked in the throat with pneumonia. I sucked it out." Then I told his mother to give him a drink of water. He drank it, and looked around. Then I said that they shouldn't feed him too much, and that I had a soup for him that they should give him when he called for it. That night around 2 o'clock in the morning he called out to his mother for something to eat. Then she gave him the soup. Next morning I saw him again, and he was sitting up. "Well," I said, "Now you can walk around again. He is a man now; Jim Payne."

John cured a medicine man. The white doctors had put Tilton West on the operating table, stretched him out and tied him fast so that he could not move around. They tried to give him ether to put him out, but they didn't succeed. He said, "Don't use it on me, just go ahead and work." The doctors used three knives but they couldn't cut into him, the knives just bent. Tilton then visited John. "It still hurts in my left side," he said. "John, I am pretty sure that you are the man who can cure me. When you take it out, I want to see it." That night John sucked it out. It was as big as the top part of the thumb joint. John then put it on the floor. It was a bag of green stuff. John did not open it, but threw it away. Tilton said, "lots of times I have vomited this out and then felt better but this time it hurt me too much." When the white doctor saw Tilton walking around town he asked him, "how do you feel?" "Pretty well," answered Tilton. "How did you get well?" asked the doctor. Tilton answered. "I can't tell you!"

A Story about *Pauagap* – Pearl Cody

One day *Pauagap*[5] went down to Bull Lake with a fishing line and hook to catch fish for dinner. *Pandzita:ygö* – her first husband, rode on horseback to the mountains to dig up *yamp?* – wild carrots. He came to a place where there were some wild carrots and dug them up. Then he heard a sound from above: krrr, krrr, krrr. He looked up and saw some cranes *–kú:indata?* – fly towards him. They slowly flew down and settled near him. "Hey, *Pandzita:ygö,"* they said. "What are you doing?" "Trying to get some *yamp?* for dinner," he answered. "Throw them out," said the cranes. *Pandzita:ygö* was confused. "What shall I do then?" he asked. "We'll take you to a better country, so you can get bigger *yamps,* said the cranes. "How big?" "As big as your thumb. Tie your sack onto your belt, we'll help you get there and dig up the *yamp?s.* We'll take you between us, and when you are high up, we'll put wings on you." "Well," said *Pandzita:ygö, if* that is so, yes, I'll go with you."

They flew up holding him between them; they went over the mountain and came to a land in the west. Then they started to go down in wide circles, saying "krrr, krrr, krrr," and told him to repeat what they were saying at the same time. "Now," they said, "you see that river where that burnt timber is." They flew there and circled once more before landing. He saw that there were very big *yamp?s* growing there. "Now," said the cranes. "You don't need sharp sticks to dig, just pull them out." He pulled and the birds helped him, and the pile grew. Soon it was a very big pile, so he put the *yamp?s* in his sack; and the whole sack was full. The cranes told him to put the sack on his back so that he wouldn't lose it. He did as they

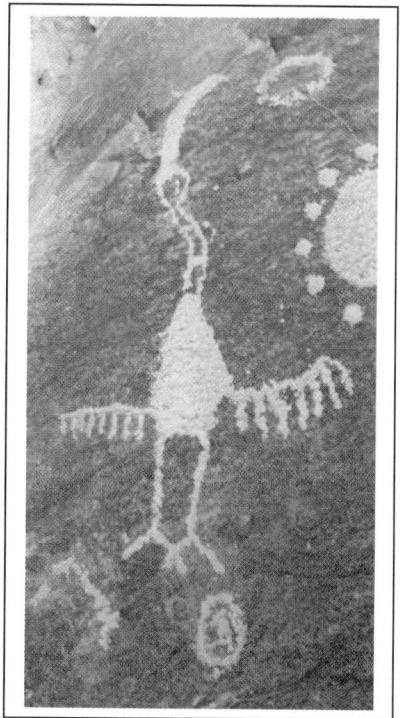

told him to do. "Let's go," said the cranes and they flew off.

They flew back toward the east and they said "krrr, krrr, krrr," as they flew and *Pandzita:ygö* did the same. Soon he looked down and saw his little white horse, still standing at the tree where he had tied it earlier. He looked towards the lake where he saw his woman cooking something. When they landed, the cranes said to him: "Whenever you want carrots, put up a red flag, and we'll come for you." *Pandzita:ygö* went home. "Where have you been all day?" asked *Pauagap*. "In Idaho," he answered. "Have you been to Idaho and back so quickly?" she said in an astonished voice. "Well," he said, "you saw the cranes. They took me there, helped me dig these carrots and brought me back again." "Let me see those carrots," said *Pauagap*, who didn't believe him! He opened the sack and showed her the contents. "Oh, that's good, you are no liar, that's true!" she said. She took the *yamp?s,* split them in half, and threw them into the soup. She was still very surprised by what had happened. "But I can't call you a liar," she said, "You don't get that kind of stuff here."

The day after this had all happened Little Bob, the father of Tudy Roberts' (a well-known medicine man), came to visit. He lived at Crowheart. *Pandzita:ygö* said to *Pauagap*, "Give him some of the carrots that I brought over from Idaho yesterday." "Where did you get those carrots?" asked Little Bob. "The cranes took me there and back," said *Pandzita:ygö*. "They also helped me to dig them up."

Later on Little Bob went to the Agency to get his ration, and had a few carrots in his pocket. Outside the building a bunch of men were sitting telling stories. "Hey, you guys, what do you think of this," said Little Bob. "I got these carrots from *Pandzita:ygö,* and he dug them up in Idaho; the cranes took him there, and also helped him to come back." They called over to *Pandzita:ygö*, who was close by. "Is this true what Little Bob says?" they asked. "Yes," he said, "that's what the birds have done for me, it's a true story." "Well," said the men, "somebody might have given them to you." "No," he said, "my wife will tell you too." The men, who wanted to call him a liar, didn't know what to say. "Well," said *Pandzita:ygö, "*if two of you fellows go with me I'll prove it." Two of the men agreed to go with *Pandzita:ygö*, and if the story was true they said that they would give him $20. "All right," said *Pandzita:ygö*, "I want to see you boys come with me on Monday." On the following Monday the two fellows turned up, and early in the morning they went up the mountain with *Pandzita:ygö*, put up a red flag, and soon the cranes arrived shrieking "krrr, krrr, krrr." "There they come," said *Pandzita:ygö*. But the birds didn't stop, they just carried on.

"Well," he explained, "they are suspicious because you boys are here. If you had not been here they would have stopped.

A Story by, "Steps-in-hole,"- *Dánboho?tzi,* another famous Story Teller

One day **Dánboho?tzi** was riding home from a hunting trip with too much elk meat packed on four or five horses; but he still wanted to have some fish. He came to a creek and thought: "Well, this is a good place to make camp, I'll let the horses rest and fish a little." He went down to the creek and took off his "chaps."[6] Then he started to fish down at the shore of the creek. After a while he said, "Well, eight fishes, that's enough." He turned round and looked behind him. "Who is that with my chaps and my hat on? A bear was standing there with *Dánboho?tzi's* hat on his head, revolver belt round his waist, and chaps on his legs! "Hey, what are you doing with my stuff on?" called *Dánboho?tzi.* "If you are a real bear, you would not put that on."

Two Indians came riding out of the forest, and at the same time *Dánboho?tzi* called out to the bear: "You better take off that outfit!" One of the Indians, who was his cousin of *Dánboho?tzi* said: "Hey, what's that bear doing with your clothes on?" "He put them on while I was fishing," answered *Dánboho?tzi. "*That's strange, said his cousin, Tom Ute, "I have never seen a bear do that." They took the clothes off the bear and all three of them rode home talking about the bear. "What made that bear do that?" they asked each other. Other Shoshone Indians later asked Tom Ute if it was true that the bear had put on the whole outfit. "Yes," said Tom, "that's true, we have seen it. The only thing that he didn't do was to saddle up his horse!"

A Story about *Kïnyakwíagan* – "he has a little hawk for his pet"[7]

Kïnyakwíagan was a young man, a camp leader. One day, early in the morning he said to his father: "I wish you could make me a boat." The father said, "after the boat has been made, where will you go?" *Kïnyakwíagan* said, "I want to go down the river to see my grandmother who lives there. I don't like my sister." "Why do you want to go to your grandmother there," asked his father. He answered, "I want to stay with her; I don't like the way my sister treats me here." "Well," said the father, "I will make a boat for you tomorrow."

The very next morning *Kïnyakwíagan* and his father went to work. The father made the boat, and *Kïnyakwíagan* helped him; he gathered wood, and carried some dirt and put it in the middle of the boat, so that he could make a fire there. His father asked him, "what are you going to do with your hawk?" *Kïnyakwíagan* said, "I want to take him with me, he is my *puha* – power."

The following morning *Kïnyakwíagan* went off. He went down the river, a mighty big river, and sailed and sailed. In the afternoon his sister came out from the water and sat herself in the boat. The little hawk shrieked. *Kïnyakwíagan* looked back and saw his sister sitting there with the hawk fighting her. "Get out of here," shouted *Kïnyakwíagan,* "I don't want you to come with me, I don't like you." "Well," said the sister, "I'm going back to the camp, and I will kill everyone there." *Kïnyakwíagan* replied, "When I return I will kill you if you have killed them." The sister disappeared into the water. She went back and killed all the members of the camp, except for their father, mother and grandmother. The grandmother that *Kïnyakwíagan* was on his way to was his mother's aunt.

Next morning, at daybreak he arrived at her camp and went into her tipi. The old woman asked, "Grandson where do you come from?" "I have come from home," he replied. "Well, I will cook you some breakfast," she said. "While you are doing that I will go outside and have a look around your camp," said *Kïnyakwíagan*. The grandmother said, "Don't stay too long *Kïnyakwíagan*, for it is dangerous here. The chief doesn't want any young men to stay outside too long; he calls them under the bluff over there, and then kills them." "Why is that so?" he asked. "Because he is jealous," she replied. "He has a very good-looking wife and all the boys are after her, and he doesn't like that." "I want to see her," said *Kïnyakwíagan*, but his grandmother said: "I warn you, don't stay outside too long, for he is no good."

He went outside, and after a little while he saw a woman coming out of the chief's tipi. She was carrying water buckets, and passed him on his way to the river. "Eh, lady," said *Kïnyakwíagan*, "please let me drink from your bucket. She let him do so, and the chief saw it. The chief was a buffalo (metaphorically), and his name was *Kedžoniatai* –"no good for anything". He came out of his tipi, and ran after *Kïnyakwíagan.* The chief said, "You have made me mad. After breakfast you come up to that red bluff for a fight with me. We'll find out who can win this fight." The grandmother said, "Grandson, I told you not to go there; now he is after you." "Well," said *Kïnyakwíagan,* "we will see how this works." The people in the tipis asked each other in low voices: "Who is this *Kïnyakwíagan?*" One old fellow said, "I think that he is the leader of that big camp up the river. He is a good man; he has got a lot of power. I bet he can kill our chief. This *Kïnyakwíagan* is a powerful man."

Right after breakfast *Kïnyakwíagan* went to the red bluff. He called his hawk to his side. *Kïnyakwíagan* took one tail feather, one plume, and one wing feather. *Kedžoniatai* made a jump at him, but *Kïnyakwíagan* jumped up in the air, and the chief hit his head on the rock. He backed away, and then *Kïnyakwíagan* blew the tail feather into the chief's mouth, so that he became weaker. "Well, *Kïnyakwíagan,* let's try it again," said *Kedžoniatai.* He made another run, but, *Kïnyakwíagan* jumped once more into the air, and the chief missed him again. Now *Kïnyakwíagan* blew the plume into the chief's mouth. It went through him and came out at his rear end, very bloody. "Well, *Kïnyakwíagan,* it looks like you have hurt me already. Even if I am hurt, I will still get you."

By this time *Kedžoniatai* was pretty weak, but he made another jump at *Kïnyakwíagan.* But *Kïnyakwíagan* jumped up in the air, and *Kedžoniatai* missed him again. *Kïnyakwíagan* blew the wing feather, into *Kedžoniata's* mouth, and he fell down dead. *Kïnyakwíagan* had killed that wicked man!
The people were very happy and said to *Kïnyakwíagan,* "good for you; we are glad to see him dead." They tore down *Kedžoniata's* tipi, and burned it to the ground. The old fellow had won his bet. He said, "that's what I told you, he, [*Kïnyakwíagan*] is a powerful man. People in the west say that he is a strong puhagant. That *kïni* – (chicken hawk), beside him is his wonderful *puha.* He is a powerful young man." *Kïnyakwíagan* married *Kedžoniata's* woman. The grandmother said, "Well, I am glad that you killed that horrible *Kedžoniata.* Listen to the people singing around the camp praising you, saying what a great young man you are." The people wanted him to stay and be their chief. But he said, "No, I have people in my big camp up the river, and they depend on me. I can't let them down. Now that I have a wife I am going home. You people here should pick someone from your own camp to be your leader. Grandmother, I will return home and I will take this woman, my wife, with me."

After they had eaten breakfast, *Kïnyakwïagan* and his wife left for home up the river. "How far are we going?" asked his woman. *Kïnyakwïagan* answered, "It will take all day and all night; we will arrive at my father's home at sunrise. She said, "What are you going to do with your kïni?" He replied, "He will stay with me." "Where does he sleep?" she asked. "Right there by my head." "Well, that's good," said his woman.

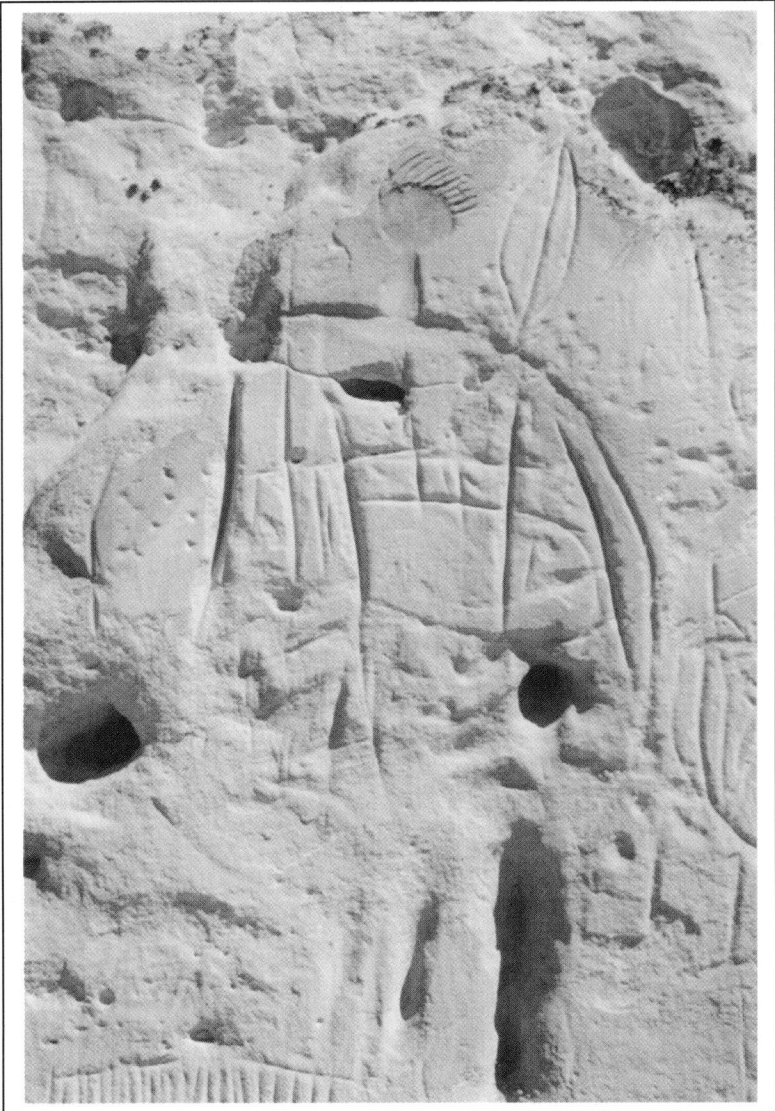

They sailed all day and all night, and at sunrise they arrived at his father's home. The woman said, "are we there now?" His mother came out to see what all the noise on the river was. She called to *Kïnyakwíagan's* father, saying, "This boy has a woman with him, come out and see." The father came out, and said, "Oh, our boy is married now!" The real grandmother came out and said, "Grandson, I am glad that you are home again. How did you get hold of that woman?" *Kïnyakwíagan* answered, "She was *Kedžoniata's* wife. He wanted to kill me and tried to do so, but I killed him first." "Did your other grandmother see you do that?" asked his grandmother. "Yes," he said, "she was there watching me."

Kïnyakwíagan asked where his sister was. His father said, "Your sister killed everybody over there in the camp. Now she is in the mountains." "Well, father," said *Kïnyakwíagan,* "give me four arrows; a yellow one, a red one, a green one, and a white one." "What are you going to do with the four arrows?" asked his father.

Kïnyakwíagan said, "I will show you what I am going to do with those four arrows. Father you come with me, I am going to make my people come to life again." "Oh," said his father, "I didn't know that you could do that." "Well, I am going to try it," said *Kïnyakwíagan.* "What are you going to do with your sister?" asked the father. *Kïnyakwíagan* replied, "When she comes back I will kill her and throw her in the water so that she can become a water baby." He took the four coloured arrows and his bow, and said, "I am going to shoot four times." First he took the yellow arrow and shot it up in the air; it started to fall down. He said, "Look out, look out, it might hit you!" The dead people started moving their toes. "Here goes the red arrow," said *Kïnyakwíagan,* and shot it off. When it came down, he said, "look out everybody, look out!"

The dead now started moving their knees. Then he sent off the third arrow. "Here goes the green arrow," he said. "I want to see everybody move. Look out, look out!" Now the dead started moving up to their waist. Finally, he shot off the fourth arrow, and said, "Here goes the white arrow. Everybody get up onto his or her feet. Look out, look out!" All the dead rose, and went over to him to shake his hand. His father said, "*Kïnyakwíagan,* you are wonderful!"

They heard the wind blowing in the mountains, and his father said, "Well, it blows that way when your sister is coming home." *Kïnyakwíagan* and his father went back to the tipi.

Then the sister came out of the woods and entered the tipi, and said to *Kïnyakwíagan:* "Why did you want to return here? We don't need you, and why have you got married? I don't like it."

Kïnyakwíagan took an arrow out of his *húguna?* - arrowsack (koger), that he had on his back, aimed the arrow at his sister and said, "this is the last time that you talk that way to me." Their father didn't say a word, for he knew that his daughter was a bad woman, and she was also a *puhagant.*

Kïnyakwíagan shot off the arrow at her, and killed her. Then he took her to the water and threw her in. "Now you are going to be the mother of the water-babies," he said; "you will be their creator." She kept crying every night in the water. The second night that she was crying *Kïnyakwíagan* went down to the river, and told her to leave that place. "You are too mean to the people!" he said.

Story of the Bear Cub

One day a girl was washing something next to the river. She was the chief's daughter. While she was washing a great big bear came and took her away up into the mountains to a cave there. She lived with that bear some four to six years, and gave birth to a little bear cub. The little bear grew up to be a boy, although he was also a bear for he was covered in fur, but he could talk.

When he was six years old, he asked his mother, "Why is it that you are a human and father is a bear?" His mother replied, "Your grandfather lives way down in the valley, he is the chief of his tribe and I am his daughter. The bear stole me away from my home." The bear boy said, "mother, let's go and see grandfather some day." "No," she replied, "we can't, your father will kill us if we go." "No," said the son, "we'll run away from him when he goes on a hunting trip." "That's a good idea," said the mother. "You find out when he is leaving to hunt, then let me know, and we'll go away when he has left." One day the old bear said to his son, "I am going away to hunt for four days. If you run away while I am not here, I will kill both you and your mother." "Oh, father," said the young cub, "I don't think that we will run away." "You better not," said the old bear, "I'm just warning you!" He then went away, leaving a rock in front of the cave's entrance.

Next day the cub moved the rock out of the doorway so that he and his mother could get out. Then he put back the rock just as it had been when the old bear left. They hurried on down to the river until they came pretty close to the chief's house. The bear mother had no clothes on, and no moccasins. The chief's wife looked out and saw the two down by the river and said to her husband, "there is somebody down at the river. It looks like our daughter and she has a little bear with her." "Go and see who it is," said the chief. She went out and soon came back. "It's our daughter," she said, "and she has a little bear cub for a son!" She got out some clothes and took them over to her daughter, who put them on and went up to the house. She shook hands with her father and her father shook hands with the cub. "What's your name?" he asked. "My name is Bear Cub – *Wúrandú:a,* or *Aguandú:a,*" answered the boy. After a while the father Bear arrived and wanted to kill his wife and son; but Bear Cub's grandfather managed to kill the old bear. The little boy played around the house.

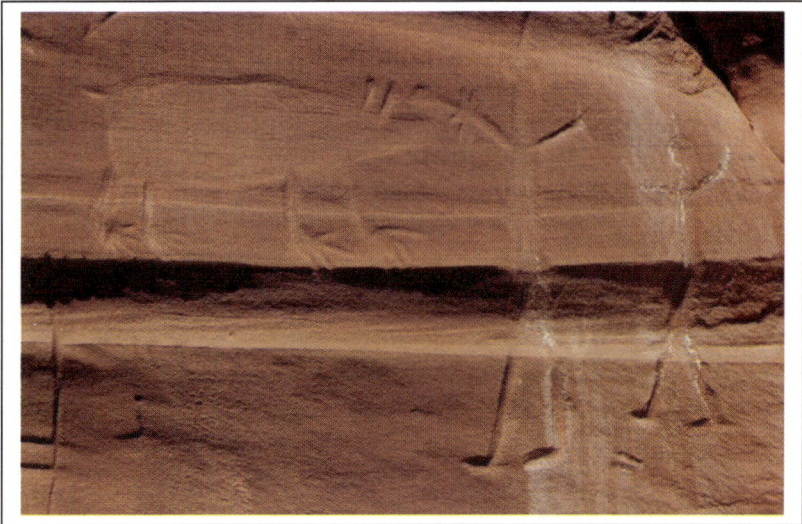

One morning he said, "Grandpa, make a cane for me, out of iron." The grandfather made a cane for him. "No, Grandfather," he said, "that cane is too small." "How big do you want it then?" asked the grandfather. "I want it about as thick as my arm," said the boy. "What are you going to do with it?" said the grandfather. "I just want to play with it," answered the boy. The grandfather made it for him and put on a handle. The boy swung it around.

His grandfather said, "That looks good, I also want to try it. "Here you are," said the boy and handed it over to his grandfather. But it was too heavy and he dropped it on his toe. "You hurt me!" the old man said. "Well," said his grandson, "you asked me for it, why blame me? Grandfather, I want to ask you for something else." "Go ahead," said the grandfather. "I want some food to take with me when I go up into the mountains. I am going up there to see Golden Moustache." Now that was the name of a chief who lived in the mountains. "Alright, Bear Boy," said the grandfather.

The young cub took his cane, and packed all kinds of stuff to eat. "Mother," he said, "I will be back some day. If I like the people there, I will stay with them, but I will first come back and let you know." "Alright my boy, but just be careful," said his mother. He went away.

After a while he saw a man who was pulling up trees with his hands. "Hello," said the boy. "Hello Bear Cub," the man answered. "Are you the grandson of the chief down here?" "Yes, that's my grandfather." "I wonder if I could go with you?" said the man. "Alright," said Bear Cub, "come right along. What's your name?" "My name is Pulling Cotton Trees," said the man. They travelled together, walking along. Then the Bear Cub said, "Let's have dinner." Bear Boy started making coffee. Then he said, "well, Cotton Tree, sit down and eat." Cotton Tree started eating, but said, "Hey, Bear Cub, I don't think that I will eat." "Why don't you want to eat?" asked the Boy. Cotton Tree replied, "There is not much food here, it is not enough for both of us." "Oh, there is more than we need," said Bear Boy. Cotton Tree began to eat and as he ate more and more food appeared. After dinner they smoked and then started off on their journey again.

In the middle of the afternoon, they saw another man who was digging out rocks. "Here is a man who is working here," said Bear Cub. "Perhaps we can get some information from him. "Yes," said Cotton Tree, "he knows what we want to know." "Hey, friends! Where are you going?" said the man. "Well," said Bear Cub. "We are going to see the man with the golden moustache. "Oh, I know him," said the man. "He is a pretty bad fellow. He does not allow outsiders to enter his camp, and before you get there you have to pass a guard first." "You are very welcome to go with us, if you wish," said Bear Cub. "What is your name?" "My name is Pulling Out Rocks," said the man, "and I would like to go with you. "Well," said Bear Cub, "let's go down here and eat some supper, then we can leave." They went along talking about Golden Moustache and came to the creek where they built a fire and cooked some stuff to eat. But Rockpuller said, "Hey, I think that I had better not eat, there is not enough food for all of us." "No, you better eat," said Cotton Tree. "There's more than you can eat here." "Well, if that's the case, I'll try it." He sat down to eat and there was plenty of food; they could not eat it all.

After they were satisfied Bear Cub said, "Let's get going on our journey so that we get somewhere before nightfall, and have time to build a house." "We are not far from our goal, said Rockpuller. "The guard that we have to pass is nearby." "I have never been in this part of the country," said Bear

Cub, "but I would sure like to live here. Hey, there is a man working there in the timber. Maybe he knows what we want to know. The man asked, "Where do you come from?" "We come from the valley," Bear Cub answered. "And where are you going?" "We are going to see Golden Moustache, and you are welcome to go with us if you would like to." What's your name?" "My name is Pinetree Puller," said the man. "Alright, come with us. We could build a house pretty quick now as there are four of us to do it." They came to a creek again, and started eating supper. Pinetree said, "I don't want to eat. There isn't enough food for all of us." "You better eat," said Rockpuller, "We have more than we need." They all ate, and there was more food than they could finish. Pinetree then said, "I want to tell you what I have heard about Golden Moustache: he is a bad man who always wants to kill newcomers; you have to have a good reputation to live in his camp." "Oh," said Bear Cub, "I have a good reputation, but I am worried about you men who are with me. Let's hurry on to the forest at the lake. We could build a house there."

They went into the forest, cut some timber, and built a house. Later on they sat around the fire inside the house. Bear Cub said, "Say, we need some meat tomorrow. Three of us will go out and get some meat. You, Cotton Tree will stay here in camp and cook for us, so that we don't have to do that when we return." "Alright, I am glad to do that," said Cotton Tree.

Next morning they went out hunting. After a while somebody knocked at the door. "Come in," said Cotton Tree, and the person entered. He was a wild-looking man with an iron hat, clothes and moccasins of gold, and he had a long moustache. "I want to eat," he said. "No," said Cotton Tree, "I can't feed you. This food is for the hunters when they return." "But I insist on eating!" said the stranger. "No, you can't have any food," replied Cotton Tree. "Do you know to who you're talking to?" said the man angrily." "I am Golden Moustache." "I don't care," said Cotton Tree bravely. "If you don't give me some food, I will knock you on the head!" "You just try it!" commented Cotton Tree. Then Golden Moustache started fighting him, and knocked him down. Then he ate as much as he wanted, and went away. After a while Cotton Tree came to, put a bandage around his head and went to bed. Now the hunters, who had not seen any game, returned. Bear Cub saw Cotton Tree in bed and said, "Hey, what's the matter with you?" "Oh, I have been down in the camp, but I fell and cut my head," lied Cotton Tree. Bear Cub said, "Well, we'll see if we can get some game tomorrow morning. Rockpuller, you can stay at home and cook for us then."

After breakfast the next morning they went out, and Cotton Tree put a cap on his sore head. Bear Cub said, "Hey, I'll tell you something, we'll have to go back pretty quick; I don't see any tracks here. We better not stay too long in the forest." In the afternoon when Rockpuller was cooking, Golden Moustache entered the hut. "Hey, I want food," he said. "You can't have any, this food is for the hunters when they return," Rockpuller replied. "Don't you talk to me that way," said Golden Moustache, "Don't you know who I am? I am Golden Moustache." "I don't care," said Rockpuller, and they started fighting. Golden Moustache knocked Rockpuller out, ate up the food, and went away. "Say, what's the matter with you?" said Bear Cub when he saw Rockpuller in bed with a bandage on his head. Rockpuller replied, "Oh, I just went down to the camp and bumped my head on a piece of wood." Bear Cub said, "Pine Tree, you had better stay in camp and cook what we have got here." "Alright," said Pine Tree, "I'll cook something."

The next day when three of them were out hunting Golden Moustache knocked on the door. "Come in," said Pine Tree. "I want food," said the chief. "You can't have any," said Pine Tree. "This food is for the hunters when they return." "But don't you know that I am the Golden Moustache! If you don't give me food I will fight you." "Try it," said Pine Tree. Then the chief attacked him, knocked him stiff, and ate as much as he wanted and went away. After a while the hunters came back and found Pine Tree in bed, with a bandage on his head. "Say, what's the matter with you?" said Bear Cub. "Oh," Pine Tree answered, "I was down at the camp, and fell and hurt myself." Cotton Tree and Rockpuller knew of course what had happened, but Bear Cub did not know. He said, "Now boys, it is my turn to cook tomorrow."

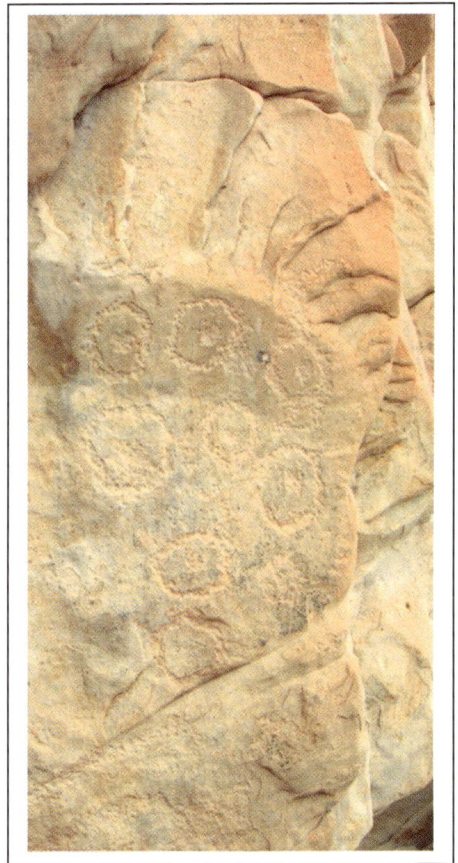

The others went out hunting the next day leaving Bear Cub to do the cooking. Now once again Golden Moustache knocked at the door, and Bear Cub said, "Come in!" The chief entered. Bear Cub said, "Well, who is this?" The man said, "I guess that you have heard about Golden Moustache." "Yes,

I have heard your name, but I have never seen you before." "Cub, I want to eat!" "No," said Bear Cub, "you can't have any food. I am cooking for the hunters." "But I want to eat," said Golden Moustache. "If you refuse to feed me, I'll knock you out, and eat what you have anyway." "Well then," said Bear Cub, "Try." He grasped hold of his cane, and when Golden Moustache went to strike him, he hit him on his back and broke all his bones, then he took him outside and killed him. Afterwards he went inside again, bandaged his head and lay down on his bed. At last the hunters returned. "Hm, hm," said Pine Tree, "I think that Golden Moustache even whipped our chief." "No," Bear Cub jumped up and laughed, "I killed Golden Moustache. I had to kill that dangerous man." The others said, "Let's have a look at him." Bear Cub went out, and showed the dead man to the hunters. All his golden stuff had been smashed in. "Well, what could I do?" said Bear Cub. "I killed him for our own protection."

Soon afterwards a stranger turned up at their camp. He was from the camp of Golden Moustache. "Which one of you killed our chief?" he asked. "The Bear did," the hunters answered. The man went on to say, "We want a chief back at our camp and you are good. You saved us from this killer, so Cub, we would like to make you our chief." So from then on Bear Cub took over the camp and made his friends into sub-chiefs – Cotton Tree, Rockpuller and Pine tree.

The story of *Tú:taivo* – black white man
This story was told to the Shoshone by French Trappers

Once there was a coloured man - *Tú:taivo*, who was out one day riding on a saddle mule. On the trail in front of him some white people were camping. "Hey, *Tú:taivo*, they said, "why do you travel so fast?" He replied, "I am going up to eat where the big camp is." "Well," they said, "it won't take you long to go there; we have been there." "How far is it?" he asked. "Oh, you might just make it by tomorrow night. Now tie up your mule, and come and eat breakfast with us." The black man tied up his mule, and washed his face and hands in the stream. Then he put on a black, magic hat, that made him invisible and no one could see him. He went over to the table with a sack, and stole some eggs and bacon. Then he went back to his mule and took off his magic hat. The people said, "*Tú:taivo*, sit over here, here is a plate for you." He sat down and ate. When he had finished he said, "well, thank you folks for breakfast and for the information." He got on his mule and loped along, eating the stolen stuff on the way. He came to where another family were making camp. They said, "*Tú:taivo*, why are you in such a hurry?" He replied. "I am travelling to the camp where they have a lot of food." "Well, you will reach there by tomorrow night. You had better stop and have dinner with us." He tied up his mule, put the black hat on, and went to see what there was on the table. He saw that there were very good things to eat, and he decided to pack some of the things in his sack, then he took it back to the mule. After he had taken off his magic hat he joined the others and said to his host, "very good of you, my friend!" Then he sat down to eat. After finishing the meal he said, "thank you for dinner and for the information. However, as I want to be there by tomorrow noon, I should leave now."

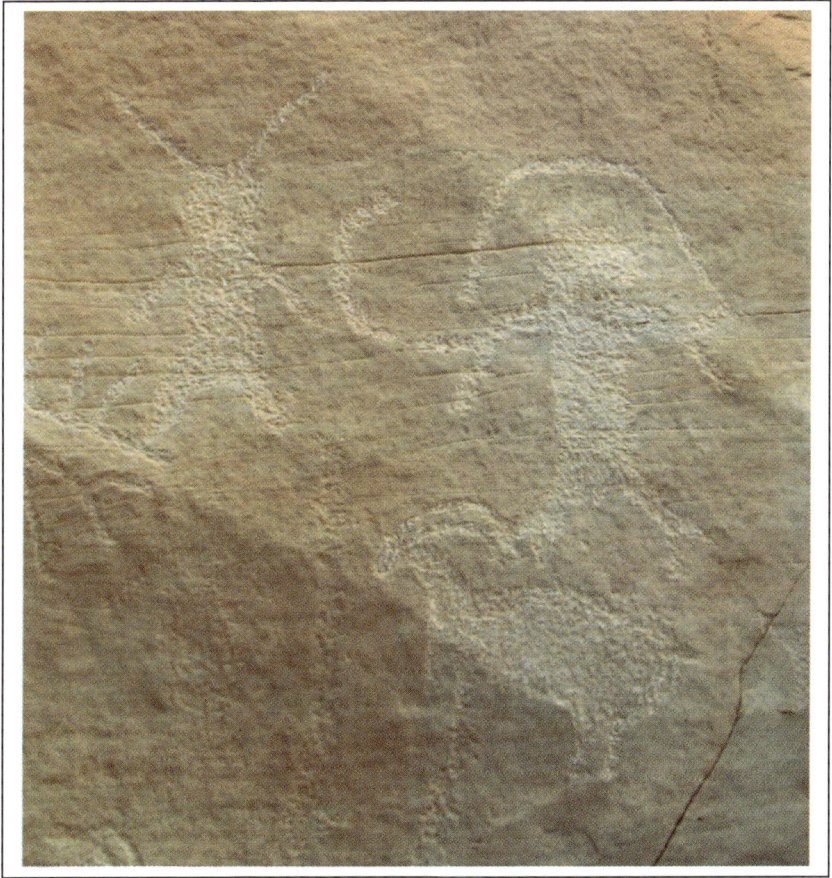

He left on his mule, and as he went along he ate the stuff that he had taken from the table. He looked up the valley and saw a trail of dust at the creek. "Oh," he said, "I'll go there, I might be lucky and get some more stuff!" He arrived at the camp. "*Tú:taivo,*" said the people there, "where are you going?" "Oh, I am going to where the big camp is." "Well, come and sit down and eat with us," they said. Then he put on his magic hat once again and went down to the supper table. He grabbed a good deal of the food and thought that he would have another meal before he went to bed. Then he went back to his mule, took off his hat, and returned to the table, sat down

73

and ate. "Thank you folks for supper," he said. "I think that I should leave now so that I can arrive at the big camp by noon tomorrow." "Oh, you can't make that," said the people. "Oh, yes," he said, "I think that I can arrive there in time for dinner at noon." He loped off.

After a while he became sleepy, and rode down to a creek. He tied up his mule, ate up all the stuff that he had taken from the table, and went to bed. Early next morning he saddled up his mule, and started off towards the mountains. Some white folk were camping along the road. "Hey, *Tú:taivo,*" they said. "What's the big rush?" "Oh, I am just going up to where the big camp is." "Well, you better sit down first and have some breakfast with us." Once again *Tú:taivo* put on his magic hat that made him invisible, put some food in his sack and then stored it away where the mule was tied up. Then he returned to the breakfast table, ate with the people and afterwards said, "Well thank you friends." "When do you want to be there?" they asked. "Oh, by noon," he replied. "You can't make it by noon, for it's a long way from here." "Oh, I will ride fast," he said. He got up on his mule and carried on his way. He soon went up a hill and saw a very big camp: there were lots of wagons, and in the middle there was a fire where they were cooking. A man came into the middle of the trail. "What are you doing?" he asked. *Tú:taivo* answered, "I have come to this big camp to eat. "No," said the man, "I don't think that they want you there." "Oh, yes," said *Tú:taivo* "I was invited to come." "Oh, no," said the man. "This dinner is for the big shots, they don't want you here." "Oh," said *Tú:taivo,* "I am one of the big shots." Then he got off his mule, and tied it up, put on white clothes and took out a cane, then put a bouquet of flowers in his jacket. He thought that he would have a look around, and then get his black hat. The people said, "Where does this fellow come from? It's certain that he was not invited to this dinner. Still, he must be representing someone, otherwise he would not be carrying a bouquet of flowers in his jacket. Meanwhile *Tú:taivo* fetched the sack and put on his black hat, filled the sack with turkey, chicken and bread and then took it back to where the mule was tied up. He returned and they said, "Well, the bell has rung, all you men walk in and take your seats." *Tú:taivo* was at the end of the table. Somebody got up and offered a prayer. All the men had their hats hanging in the hall and *Tú:taivo's* magic hat was also hanging there.

There were some little boys playing around, and they went into the hall, and took everybody's hat with them, including the magic one. After half an hour the big shots had finished eating and were going off to talk. *Tú:taivo* went out into the hall, and found that there were no hats there. He had lost his hat! The kids were playing with the hats and *Tú:taivo* said, "It is too bad that I lost my hat, that's the only protection that I've got." At the meeting they missed *Tú:taivo,* and one fellow said, "where is *Tú:taivo?*" "I don't know,"

74

said another. "Well, we'll have to punish him for not being here," said the first man. *Tú:taivo* was back with the mule and felt sad. "I wonder why I hung up my hat in that hall? How stupid of me!" he said to himself. He rolled out his bed under an old pine tree and went to sleep.

The next morning when he got up he looked down the ridge and saw that there were a lot of antelopes going to the water. It appeared that everybody had moved away and he seemed to be alone there. He went down to the creek and the Buck Antelope went over to him. "Don't shoot me and I will tell you good news," he said. "Alright," said *Tú:taivo,* "tell me quick or I will shoot you." The Buck Antelope said, "There are three girls swimming in the pool over here. You take the dress that you see is in the middle and that will give you a good woman, for she is a very good woman. Those three girls are the daughters of the ogre - *Nïmïrika.* But don't you give up her dress until you get her ring, then she will be yours." *Tú:taivo* crawled down to the shore, took the dress that was in between the other two, and ran away with it.

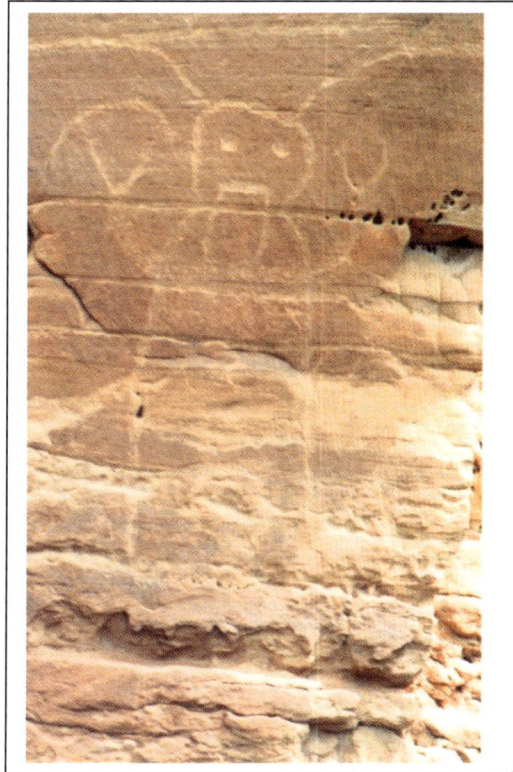

The sister whose dress he had taken was still in the water, and when she discovered that he had taken her dress she said, please *Tú:taivo* give me back my dress." He answered, "I will give you your dress if you give me your ring." "No!" she said. "My father gave me this ring, and he is a dangerous man. He will eat you up if you don't give me back my dress." "Oh, no he won't" said *Tú:taivo* convincingly. "Well," she said, "I will hold this ring until you give me my dress." Still, he was firm and said, "no, you take that ring off your finger and give it to me and I will give you your dress." She gave in and gave him the ring and said, "I never want you to refuse me anything again!" He pushed the ring on his finger and gave her back her dress. "Now we are married," he said. "Where do you live *Tú:taivo?"* she asked. "Oh," he explained. "I have no house, but I have my

75

outfit and my mule by that pine tree." "That's alright," she said. "I will camp with you outside tonight. They both went up to where the pine tree was and *Tú:taivo* said: "I really wish that we were back where I have a nice house and lots of comforts. If I also had my magic black hat, everything would be perfect."

They slept there that night and in the morning *Tú:taivo* woke up and looked around and found out that they were at his home. His wish had come true! "My chickens and cows are all here, even my dogs are here. My wife and I will be happy here in our good home. Well, I am glad that my *puha* took me home through my wishes. Woman! get up and cook breakfast for me. When it is ready just give me a call and I will come in and eat."

Just a short while later his wife called him in and he ate his breakfast. Then he went out again to work hard in the field. Later on his wife called to him, "*Tú:taivo,* you need to buy more food!" He replied, "Don't you boss me around, I don't like that!" Then she cried, "I told you not to refuse me anything. I will take back the ring and return to my camp!"

That night when her husband was asleep, she pulled the ring off his finger and ran away from *Tú:taivo* and went back to her father, *Nïmïrika.* When *Tú:taivo* woke up the next morning he found that he was sleeping back under the pine tree, far away from his home. "Oh, this is no good," he wailed. "Well, I must go. She is not the right kind of woman anyhow; she is after all, part *Nïmïrika.* I think that I will saddle my mule and go down to where the other people are." He went away and after a while he saw some boys playing around the trail. A little boy said, "Say, *Tú:taivo,* give us smoke!" "Well, boys, put your hats in a row and go down 100 yards. The boy who runs fastest and who first reaches his hat will have the smoke. "This is my chance," thought *Tú:taivo* to himself. "I will take it and run away." The boys stood a little further away and asked, "Is this 100 yards here?" "No, walk further back!" said *Tú:taivo.* Then he grabbed his hat and ran off as fast as he could. The boys couldn't understand it, "where is *Tú:taivo?*" The little boy said, "He took that hat! That must have been a magic hat!" The older boys said, "That's not very good; why did you ask him for a smoke? Now we have to go home. We can't catch up with him, we can't even see him!" And that is the way that *Tú:taivo* got back his magic hat.

A story about Porcupine – *yïh* – (animal with needles)

Porcupine had a kind of *puha.* He said to his mother and father, "I am going away, but I will leave my medicine here on those tipi-poles. When I get into danger and get killed off, the medicine will fall off the pole, and then you will know that I have been killed." He went up along the river towards the mountains. When he started it was early spring. He came to some buffalo dung, and he said, "dung, when were you dropped here?" It answered, "I was dropped here just when the grass started growing.[8] "Which way did the buffalo go after you were dropped here?" asked Porcupine. "They went straight up the creek there," replied the dung. "Alright," said Porcupine and he went on his way, walking until he came to another pile of dung, and asked, "how long ago did the buffalo drop you?" The dung answered, "it was when the high water came."[9] " What direction did the buffalo take after that?" asked Porcupine. The dung said, "I think that they went straight up the river." So Porcupine continued on his journey and ran into another pile of dung that looked more recent. "When were you dropped?" he asked. The dung answered, "I think that it was at the time when the water was sinking,"[10] said the manure. "And where did they go?" asked Porcupine. "They went up alongside the river," replied the dung.

Now Porcupine went on up the river, talking to himself. "I don't think that I'll meet any danger. I think that I will be safe here." Then he saw another pile of dung. "When were you dropped?" he asked. The dung answered, "Oh, about ten days ago." "How close am I to those buffalo?" said Porcupine. "Oh, you are pretty close to them," replied the dung. "Which way did they take?" The dung answered, "When the leader swam across he dropped me. Just look across the river, you might see them." Porcupine went up on to the riverbank, and looked over at the other side. "Well," he said, "it is a little too high for me to cross. I will try to call some of them over here."

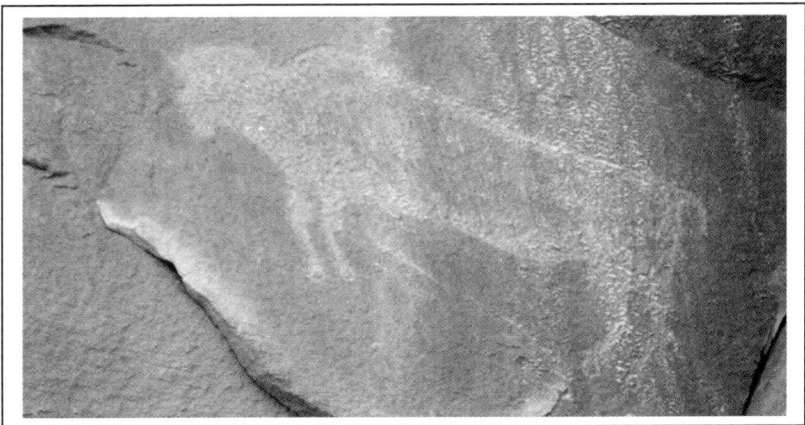

The buffalo were on the other side of the river lying in the shade of the trees. "What shall I say to them?" He put his hands to his mouth, [John demonstrated with his hands], and shouted, "that one sitting on the end, come and take me across the water."[11] One buffalo said, "No!" The

Porcupine repeated his prayer. Another buffalo said "No!" So once more Porcupine said the prayer, and again he got "no" for an answer. This was repeated until the last but one buffalo said, "No," but after that the last buffalo said "Yes!" This particular buffalo got up; it was a big, fat cow. She crossed the river. Porcupine[12] said, "Oh, that's going to be good food!" The buffalo said, "Where do you want to sit? Do you want to sit on my back, or do you want to sit on my hump?" Porcupine replied, "I don't want to sit on your back or your hump, you might shake me off into the river." "Then where do you want to sit?" asked the buffalo. "Do you want to get into my nose?" "No," said Porcupine, "you might blow your nose in the water and blow me out." "Do you want to sit in my mouth?" "No, you might spit me into the river, if you step on a sharp rock." "Do you want to be inside me, right down to my stomach?" "Yes," said Porcupine, "that would be a good place for me." So the buffalo swallowed him. Porcupine said, "When we get to the other side, let me off where there is a nice, green place. Let me know when you get there." "Alright, here we go," said the buffalo, and started to cross the river. After a while Porcupine said, "Where are we now?" "Oh," said the buffalo, "we are not half way across yet." A little later Porcupine asked, "are we in the middle of the river now?" "No, we have passed the middle," answered the buffalo. Again Porcupine asked, "Where are we now?" The buffalo replied, "Oh, we are pretty near across now." Once again Porcupine asked where they were and the buffalo said, "We are across now." "Then hunt up a good, green place," said Porcupine.

The buffalo went on until she found a nice, grassy spot. "I have to sit down to let you out, so that you won't fall," she said. Porcupine felt when she sat down. "Now we are here in the middle of a nice, green spot." Alright," said Porcupine, and then he shot his quills into the buffalo's inside. The buffalo got up and started staggering around; he kept shooting, until she fell down dead. He crawled out of her mouth. "Now, I have got something good," he said. "I will go down to the sandbar to find a sharp rock to cut the meat with. What shall I get to cut out the tongue with?"[13]

Now just then Coyote happened to be wandering up the creek and hid when he heard someone shouting out. "It sounds like Porcupine," he said. "If he yells again I will be sure who it is." Porcupine called out again "what shall I get to cut out the tongue with?" Coyote knew who that was. "Oh," he said, "That must be my nephew Porcupine. He has got something good there. I'll go up to him and find out what he has killed." Porcupine didn't see him coming, and called out the same question again.

Coyote went up behind him. "What are you saying nephew?" he asked. "Oh, I was just talking," said Porcupine. Coyote went on, "I heard you plain, I heard you saying: ʹwhat shall I get to cut your tongue out with?ʹ" "No," answered Porcupine, "you didn't hear me say that!" "Oh, yes, I heard it; you are looking for a sharp rock." "Oh, no, that's not true." "Well, what did you say then?" Coyote asked. Porcupine answered; "I said, what will I get to cut the brush with."[14] "No, Porcupine," said Coyote,"You said that you were looking for something to cut out a tongue with." "No, Coyote, you misunderstood me."

But Coyote insisted, "Oh, yes, I heard you say that." "Well, I might as well tell the truth. I killed a buffalo up here, it's good and fat. "Well, where is it?" said Coyote eagerly. "Right up there at the green spot at the bend of the river." "Oh, I see. I'll tell you nephew, what we can do. I have got a knife here. The one who jumps over the buffalo without touching it will cut up that buffalo." But Porcupine said, "No, I killed that buffalo for my own use; you just made up a plan to take it away from me."

"No, that's a deal," said Coyote. "No, that's not a deal, that isn't right. But we can divide it up: you can have half, which will be a good deal," said Porcupine. "No, jump over it," said Coyote. "The one who jumps over the buffalo without touching it will take the buffalo." "Alright," said Porcupine, "go ahead and jump!"

Coyote ran; he started to jump before he got close enough to the buffalo. He slipped, and fell on the buffalo. Porcupine said, "Oh, I have got it now, you didn't jump clear over it." Coyote said, "No, you have not jumped yet." Porcupine ran, then he jumped clear over the buffalo without touching it. But Coyote said, "it is not fair of you to take the buffalo when I slipped and fell on it. Give me another chance, let's try it again."

They argued over the deal, but finally Coyote talked Porcupine into his way of thinking: they would run again and jump. Porcupine was hoping that Coyote would fail again but he didn't. He jumped clear over the buffalo this time, whereas Porcupine slipped and fell on it. Porcupine said, "Well, you fell the first time, now I fell; so we'll divide it up." But Coyote said, "No, the deal was that the one who jumped over the buffalo without touching it would have it."

"No, I killed the buffalo, it's not right if you take it alone, we should divide it!" "Ah, but I have the knife to cut it up," said Coyote. He took out the tongue and then started cutting up the body. He cut open the paunch, took out the grass, then the "bible,"[15] and said, "Porcupine, go down to the creek and wash it. But I don't want you to eat it but bring it back to me." Porcupine carried the "bible" down to the river, and sat down on the bank and started to sing and eat. He ate up most of the it, and took the rest to Coyote.

He left the remainder a little distance away so that Coyote could not see that he had eaten anything. Coyote asked, "You didn't eat any, did you?" "No," answered Porcupine. "Well," said Coyote, "I'll just go down and ask the water bugs if you have eaten any of it." He went down to the river and asked them. "Yes," they said, "he sat on the bank here, eating and singing; he ate most of it."

"Oh, he lied to me," said Coyote, and went up again. "Hey, Porcupine," he said "the water bugs said that you ate up most of it." Then Coyote hit Porcupine on the head and knocked him out. Then he muttered to himself, "now I'll get my family here so that they can pack the meat and take it down to our camp." Porcupine just lay there. When Coyote had gone off Porcupine woke up, stood up and then walked to a place where four young pine trees were growing close together.

He made a platform on them, packed the meat, stored it there and then sat down on the platform. He started talking: "*Páwuygušö, páwuygušo, páwuygušö, páwuygušö,*" (pine trees grow up). The trees started growing, and he climbed up higher as they grew, up to a height where he knew that Coyote could not reach him. Then he watched for signs of Old Coyote and his family coming up from the valley. Then he saw Coyote coming together with his wife, boys and his two girls who were playing shinny.[16] When Porcupine saw the two girls he said, "what good-looking girls, I wish I had the chance to sleep with them. No, if Coyote had treated me right then maybe there had been a chance but now he is my enemy and I shall kill all of them."

Coyote looked around; there was no meat where it should have been. "If I catch that Porcupine," he said, "I will fix him!" The little boy, who was sitting on the back of Coyote's wife said, "Look – way up in the tree top!" Coyote looked up. "Oh," he said, "there it is, way up there! "Nephew, give me a piece of that meat!" "Well," said Porcupine, "put that baby next to the tree so he won't get hit by the meat when I throw it down. And everyone, hold up your hands to catch it." Porcupine threw down the front quarter of the buffalo down on Coyote's family, and it killed Coyote, his wife, his two daughters and his son.

Only the baby was left alive. Porcupine went down and fetched the baby and then took him back up to the platform. He had a lot of meat cooked there, and he filled the baby boy with meat. The little boy said, "I am too full up, I want to get rid of it." Porcupine said, "Well, walk out on that branch." "No," replied the little boy, "I'm afraid that I might fall off."

"No," said Porcupine, "I don't want you to do your business here, go out there." The boy walked out on the branch. "Here?" he said. "No, you are too close, you might make the meat smell." The boy went a little farther out. "Right here?" he asked. "Yes," said Porcupine, "that's far enough." Then he jerked the branch, made the little boy fall off and he fell dead to the ground. Porcupine decided to dry the best part of the meat and take it home to his mother and father.

Now when Coyote had knocked Porcupine out, his medicine (*puha)* at home fell off the pole where it had been tied. His mother and father cried and thought that something had happened to him. Porcupine knew that. He left quite a lot of meat on the platform, and said, "I will not stop and hunt now, I will hurry home, for my medicine is off the pole, and my mother and father must be worrying about me." He went home and arrived there round about sunset. His mother and father were sitting with their back towards the fire, crying. Porcupine went in, and said, "mother and father, don't cry, I am back home again." But his father said, "Oh that must be my son's ghost - *dzó:a!*" He grabbed a handful of ashes and threw it back over his shoulder into Porcupine's face saying, "go away, ghost of my boy!" "No, father," said Porcupine, "this is your son himself, it isn't my ghost. Look at me, I am not a ghost!" The father looked up, and there was his son. "Son," he said, "I am glad to see you again." Porcupine said, "I brought you some good, fat, buffalo meat." That's what we like," said his father. "But why did your medicine fall off the pole?" His son replied, "Well, when I killed the buffalo, Coyote tried to take it away from me. He hit me on the head and almost killed me." "Oh," said his father, "that's why it fell off the pole. Never trust Coyote any more, that's one person that you should never trust!"[17]

The Head in the Buckskin

There was a battle somewhere in this country and the enemies killed a girl's boyfriend, and captured the girl. About a year and a half later she managed to escape from her captors, and travelled by night. Around dawn she went right by the battlefield and happened to notice where the boy had been killed. His head and bones were lying around. She stayed there all day crying. When it started to get dark she began walking again along the trail. But the head followed her and caught up with her, and when night fell she heard a voice say, "turn off the trail, there are some enemies coming." She left the trail and hid under a juniper bush, and the head followed her and crawled up on her chest.

While she was lying there with the head she saw some riders on horseback on the trail. Then she heard the voice again: "Now get away from this hill, and go down to that little creek where you will find some horses. Take the first horse that is tied to a tree, and make your get away as fast as you can. Take me with you so that nothing can happen to you until we get home."

She did as the voice had told her and carried the head in a buckskin. Then the voice said, "You let me stay in your mother and father's house for just one night, then you must bury me, wrapped up in the buckskin." She arrived home, and let the head stay overnight, then buried it, covered in the buckskin.

The Story of Uncle Ned

Two Comanches took their horse and wagon to Oklahoma City where they bought a coffin for their Uncle Ned who had just passed away. On the way home they saw in the distance a white man on a horse. They were acquainted with him and thought that they could play a joke on him! One of the brothers took off the lid of the coffin and climbed inside. The white man came closer and saw the Comanche travelling with a coffin and said: "Oh, I heard that your Uncle Ned had died. Do you think that I could see him one last time?" "Of course," said the Comanche, and lifted off the lid of the coffin. The white man looked into the coffin and said, "Oh, Uncle Ned, when did you die?" "Yesterday!" said the body in the coffin. The white man fainted!

Story of the Three Scouts Who Didn't Follow their Leader's Instructions

At one time three scouts were going north. They were Ute Indians and their names are unknown. Before they started off their chief had said to them: "Now, boys, don't make too long a trip!"

The first day they travelled in the mountains. They hadn't taken much food with them, only enough to last for three days. They were going along the mountainside. After a day and a half they reached the top of the highest mountain that they could get to. They looked over both sides of the mountain. Their leader said, "the chief told us to make the trip short, so we had better start back now." "Well," said one of the other two, "we are not very far away." Then the third scout said, "Let's make for the next mountain and see if there are any enemies there." But the leader did not like that plan and said, "I don't see anything on either side of this mountain. Early this morning we could see camp smoke, but not anymore. There is no point in us going on any further, but if you decide to go, I will go with you."

So they went on as the other two wanted, and the next day they came to another mountain. The leader said, "well, we made it over here, and there is still no sign of any tracks; all these tracks were made early in the summer." "What shall we do now?" asked the other two scouts. "We should go back," said their leader, "as we promised our chief that we would only be away for a short trip. We must go back quickly as we haven't much food left." They figured out that it would take them two and a half days to get back to their camp.

They started on their way back and slept very well the second night for they were all very tired. The next day they started off early in the morning. One of them said, "What use is it to go over the mountain when we could cut across and shorten our journey? There are no enemies here." They cut across, as he had suggested, and arrived at a creek. One of them said, "This water looks shallow." Just then a jackrabbit jumped out of the brush and stopped. "Wait a minute," said one of the scouts, "let me kill him!" He shot and killed the animal. "Hey, let's eat him raw; I am so hungry!" The leader said, "You are not supposed to eat anything raw on a trip like this. It's *máušunt,* it causes bad luck." But the other two took no notice; they ate up the rabbit.

It was getting dark before they crossed the creek. One of them said, "Say, let's go back a little to the place where there was plenty of wood, and we can build a fire there and stay all night." But the leader said, "You guys broke the rules, and it's no good making a camp here. But that makes no difference now." He went down to the bank with them. A young water buffalo came out of the brush and went towards the creek. The two younger scouts killed the buffalo, skinned it, and started to eat it raw. The leader said, "Oh, you two! Sure enough something bad is going to happen to us; you don't listen to me and I am responsible for you." The two younger scouts made a fire, and laughed at him, and said, "You have some funny rules; We don't believe in them. When a man wants to eat, he has to eat." "Well," said the leader, "he can eat, but he should eat the right kind of stuff. You know what the old men say. You should believe in those things." "Well," said the other two, "We will find out how true it is."

It was quite dark by now, and one of the young men was sitting by the fireside. Suddenly he kicked the ground hard with his feet, although he didn't mean to do it. "Now something will happen!" said the leader. The scout, who had kicked the ground said, "Well, I feel kind of funny. Something is happening to me!" He kicked once more, then again and again. "Say," he said, "my feet are getting too warm." The leader said, "Pull off your moccasins and let us see." The scout pulled off both his moccasins.

The others looked and saw to their amazement that he now had a rabbit foot. "Now I feel something strange happening to my knees," he said. The leader said, "Roll up your leggings." He did so and they found that he now had rabbit fur on his knees. Every time he kicked the fur grew further up his leg. The last time he kicked, his head turned into the head of a rabbit. The leader said, "I told you that something bad would happen, but you didn't believe me!" The rabbit jumped up and loped off.

The other scout, who had also eaten the raw buffalo meat, was worried and said, "I am sorry that we didn't listen to you." The leader said, "You should have known better. You have been scouting for a long time; you should believe what you are told. I have been scouting for a very long time and I believe in it. That's why I am the leader now. Well, I am afraid that I will have to go back home alone, for I am still afraid that something more will happen."

The other man said, "Well, you tell the people what has happened to us, if anything else goes wrong." The leader said, "People won't believe me. They will say that you were killed. I wish that I had brought along someone else with me instead of you two young fellows." Then they went to bed, but the fire was still burning. Suddenly the young man burst out, "Brother, look at me!" The leader said, "What's the matter?" The other man replied, "Both my feet are now hooves!" "Well, what did I tell you," said the leader. "Brother," said the other one, "put a stick of wood on the fire and look at me." The leader did so, and saw that the other fellow's legs right up to his knees looked like buffalo legs. They went back to bed again. But after a while the young man called out, "brother, look at me!" The leader looked again at him; now he was buffalo right up to his waist. Again they went to bed. "Brother, look at me!" shouted the young man. The leader looked at him and saw that he was now buffalo up to his arms. "Well, boy," said the leader, "that shows that you are not a very good scout. A scout is supposed to have belief, but you didn't believe in the rules."[18] They went back to bed again. Then the young man called for the last time, "Brother, look at me!" The leader looked; the other fellow had a buffalo head and horns!

By this time it was pretty near sunrise. The leader said, "I guess that you could say that I was proved right. But the people won't believe it is true that you two boys turned into a jackrabbit and a buffalo." "You could always come back here with them, and stand on the sand bar and call my name," said the buffalo. "I am going into the water. You can come back here and kick the ground right here. I will see you again if they don't believe you when you tell them what has happened." The leader watched him until he had disappeared into the water. Then the chief scout went across the river. He kept going all day and had nothing to eat. When darkness fell he arrived at the main camp.

Somebody said, "There is just one scout back; I wonder what has happened." The announcer called the chief scout over to the camp-leader's tent. "Well, tell us the news. I understand that you have come back alone." "Yes," said the chief scout. "What's the trouble?" asked the chief. The chief scout said, "Well, we came to a river and there a jackrabbit jumped out of the brush. One of the boys killed it and ate it raw." "Oh," said the camp-leader, "don't you know the laws for scouts?" "Yes, and I told them, but they didn't believe me and didn't obey, and one of them turned into a jackrabbit." "Sure," said the chief, "that happens, and what about the other one?" "Well, he ate a water-buffalo raw, and turned into a water-buffalo. This morning he disappeared into the water. If you people don't believe me, I will take you back to the lake and call him." The chief said, "Sure, such things happen. Whenever you go against the rules you get into trouble. Still, we'll go back with you to see."

The next morning an announcement was made that everybody who wanted to go and see what had happened to the young scouts could do so. Quite a few of the people went along, and in the afternoon they arrived at the lake. They saw the tracks. The chief scout went out on the sand bar. He kicked the ground, and called the young scout's name. Then they saw something coming up out of the water; it was the water buffalo. The chief talked to him: "You boys should have lived up to the rules; you had a good leader but you didn't listen."

Notes
1.   This place was further along on the same river but higher up in the mountains than the place where he and John went with Mrs. Schultz in order to see the rock drawings.
2.   This in answer to a question from Åke Hultkrantz.

86

3. Deborah interrupted here to say that Tudy was stingy.

4. Time and time again Åke Hultkrantz asked John how he knew that he should cure the man with smoke. He always gave the same answer. "I knew it. I won't tell you more."

5. *Pauagap* (Pearl Cody), was "mad" as long as John Trehero had known her – she had had three husbands: a. *Pandzötá:ygö* ("bare spot," as for example the prairie alcali), who was also nicknamed *Tónowaygáre* ("sits on grease-wood"); he was "no good, he liked to lie, and told funny stories;" b. *Xojandísona?* ("He used a dirty plate"); c. *Názaha?ni* ("he drives/a horse/ for himself") who was nicknamed *Pá:cöngu:?* ("purple bull") and *Múmbic* ("owl").

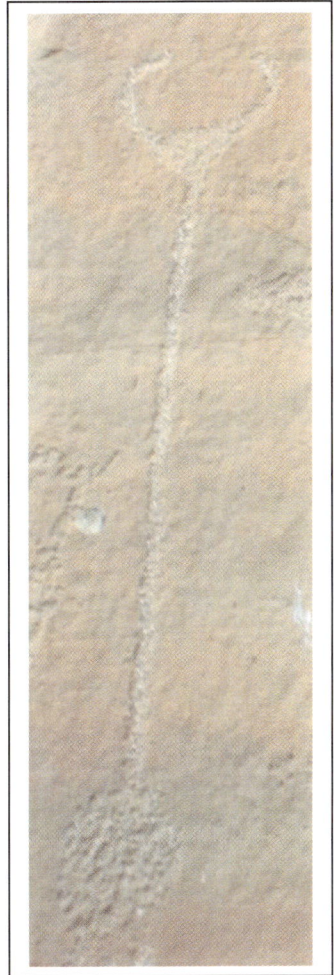

6. Chaps are leather protectors worn for riding, typical cowboy equipment.

7. "He has a little hawk for his pet," – *kïni* – meaning chicken hawk.

8. John Trehero said that this was in March.

9. This was approximately May.

10. This was around July, thought John.

11. *Ó:raygugare niö pánusare? Niö pánusare?* This prayer to carry him [Porcupine] over the water was thereby repeated.

12. Here Porcupine is called *Yïhnatsi?*

13. *Hïmawiža éigonzagwei.*

14. *Hïmawiža sïsïrakwura.*

15. According to John the so-called "bible" is a delicate titbit, from in the buffalo stomach.

16. Shinny is a "girls' game, where you hit balls with crooked sticks.

17. John says here that this was one of the stories where Coyote gets killed and yet he comes to life again in other stories. John cannot give an explanation for this. John also mentions that many of his tribesmen have told him not to tell me (Åke Hultkrantz) his stories, because they say that I am a communist! But John has told them that is not true.

18. *Šú:cixo,* "ways," is the Shoshone word for "rules."

Chapter 5

Stories about Dwarfs – *nïnïmbï*, Dragons - *bia dogwa*, Monsters – *woikaimumbic*, Cannibals/Ogres – *nïmïrïka*, and Witches - *pán-zóaváipö*.

John and Deborah Trehero told Åke Hultkrantz that they had seen two living dwarfs - *nïnïmbï* under a glass case at a circus in Denver. The dwarfs were hardly a metre tall. One was very well built with big muscles, sported a beard and loose hair that reached down to his shoulders. He had long finger-nails and had scratches on his face. He wore buckskin breeches or "shorts" but his upper part was naked. John said, "They called them pygmies. They didn't let you come close to them, as you could be scratched. There are *nïnïmbï* at Dinwoody. If you go there you mustn't say their name on the way or they might come over you."

At the same circus in Denver, "There was another bunch in the water: three water babies in a glass aquarium. They had webbed fingers, like beavers, and were long-haired; their hair went down to their knees. They were about 1.20 metres tall.

A Story of Dragons in Hot Springs
John and Deborah Trehero told this story to Åke Hultkrantz.

Dragons – *pia dogwa* (or big snakes), have been found for two to three hundred years in the Hot Springs at Thermopolis, *.pa:ygusowïnö?* (water steams) or *pa:ywíwïnö?* (big water smoke). However, there have been no dragons in Washakie Hot Springs, *tei pa:ygwíwïnö?* (little water smoke).[1] It was considered good for the health to bathe often in Washakie Hot Springs.

Many years ago some Shoshone were riding in the vicinity of Thermopolis in the direction of the Big Horn Mountains; they were on a horse-stealing expedition. It was Autumn and a little snow was falling. They stopped for a rest and a smoke at a very high point and looked over the landscape. Then they saw tracks in the snow. They rode over and found strange tracks of a creature that left the footprints of a turkey, but much larger; these tracks were "long as a man's arms." From the tracks they could make out that the creature had three toes. They followed the tracks that led to the edge of the hot springs, and there they suddenly disappeared.

A Crow Indian recalled that long ago they saw a dragon "take a buffalo in his mouth;" the buffalo seemed like a small bug in comparison with the dragon.

Nowadays they say that are no dragons left in the Hot Springs at Thermopolis. Folks say, "Maybe he is gone somewhere!" The dragon looked like a lizard, "Sawblade in the back clear to his tail." John and Deborah had seen a "mountain dragon" in Utah, roughly 20 miles from Vernal [Dinosaur National Monument]. The first time they were there the dragon was just a skeleton (bones), but the second time someone had "mounted over the bones." That particular dragon had a tail that was around 15 yards long [here John demonstrated "as from here to that pole over there!"] The tail was very thick; the dragon had short front feet and long hind legs.[2]

Stories about Man-Eaters or Cannibals – *nïmïrïka*

Some Indians were having "a big hand game" in a man's home. Two widows were in their own camp in tall grass huts, quite close by. In the moonlight the women heard horrible roars from some man-eating giant. The horrifying noise grew closer and closer. The women rushed into the men's hut and shouted "*nïmïrïka* is coming!" But the men didn't take any notice and just said, "It's only the young men playing a joke on you!" The men went on playing their game and didn't hear the *nïmïrïka*. Then it entered the hut and the men fainted. *Nïmïrïka* felt each person all over to see who was the fattest. Then he took his tomahawk and killed the two fattest men, and carried them off. When he had gone, the others "went out of fainting", and at once they wanted to move their camp: "let's get away from this place, the *nïmïrïka* are no good here." Even the women moved their huts; everybody moved.[3]

Not too long ago, [this was told to Åke Hultkrantz in the middle of the 1950's], in a battle a Shoshone woman was taken captive by some Sioux Indians. However, she managed to escape from them and wandered back to the Shoshone camp. In the evening "walking in the trail," she heard a *nïmïrïka* wailing. She hid herself behind some junipers and saw a huge, tall man come out of some rocks. That woman who told us is no longer alive.

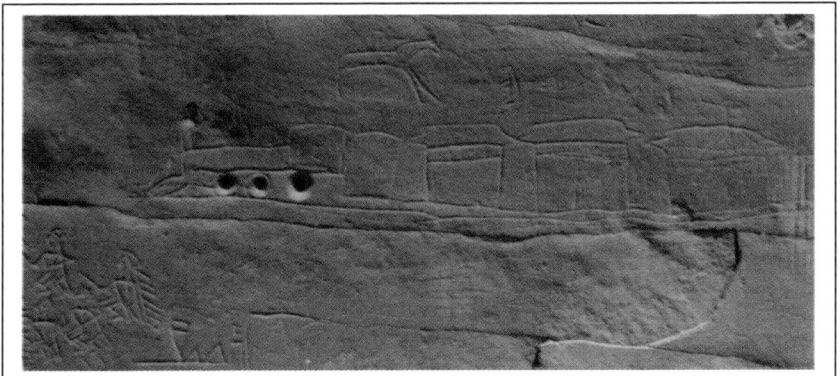

The following story is more modern, "since they made these trains." A train left Pocatello for the Sawtooth Mountains where there was a mining camp. A few Indians were on their way to Salmon City and they were in the last carriage of the train. They saw a large man run towards the train from the far hills. The closer he got, the larger he became, and he was huge. He grabbed the locomotive and tried to stop it. His feet were the size of an arm's length and he was 12 – 14 feet tall, or even taller. He almost managed to stop the train but the engine threw him off. He caught hold of it again, but his feet slipped. Three times this happened, but after the third time he gave up, and the locomotive could go on its way. "That was a *nïmïrïka.*"

An Indian Story about *Pandzó:apits* – Rock Hide[4]
(Recounted here as John Trehero told it to Åke Hultkrantz)

Óhaku:e – Yellow Crown was a King who ruled over a kingdom near a lake. One day he had a message from *Pandzó:apits,* (a type of *nïmïrïka*), that said, "If you don't feed me with a nice person, I will kill all the people in town!" The King sent back the following message: "I will give you my daughter to eat as long as you leave my people alone and don't harm them." But a young man who lived in that country was upset and said to himself, "Yellow Crown shouldn't do that.. I will save that girl, so that *nïmïrïka* cannot eat her up. I will kill that *nïmïrïka.*" Then he made his way to the home of the King and said, "Yellow Crown, I want to see your daughter." Yellow Crown replied, "You can't see her now, she's in that room there, where *nïmïrïka* is going to eat her up." The young man protested, "No, he's not going to eat her up, I'm going to take her away from him." Yellow Crown said, "You can't take her away now, I have given her to *nïmïrïka.*" However he allowed the young man to go into the room and talk to his daughter. The young man said, *"Nïmïrïka* can't eat you up. I'll save you. He will have to eat me up first."

The girl was wearing a ring and he said to her, "Give me the ring." She took it off and gave it to the young man. When *nïmïrïka* entered the room, the young man stood there with his "pets:" fox, mink and jackrabbit; they were his *púha* - power. "What are you in here for?" asked *nïmïrïka.* "Well," said the young man. "If you can kill me first, you can eat up the girl." *Nïmïrïka* had seven heads! He said, "Alright, we'll make a mark here, a line. If I pull you over to the other side of the line, I'll eat you up, and then I'll eat the girl." It was to be a sort of tug-of-war battle. They started to fight and pull. First the fox jumped into *nïmïrïka's* mouth. Then the mink went and then the jackrabbit. They had jumped into the mouth of the smallest head. The largest head was situated in the middle. The fox ran right through the body, cutting it as he went along and he came out at the rear end. The mink did the same and then so did the jackrabbit. The young man then quickly took his sword and cut off the smallest of the heads."[5] "*Nïmïrïka* said, "Let's take a little rest." Now of course he still had six heads left, but he was breathing heavily and his chest was heaving up and down violently. "Well, boy," he said at last. "Let's try again!" They started to fight once more and then fox, followed by mink and jackrabbit ran through the body again. The young man then took up his sword and struck off another head. "Mm," said *nïmïrïka,* "he has only left me with five heads, let's take a break." They rested for a short while then *nïmïrïka* said lets start fighting again. Once more the fox, then the mink and the jackrabbit jumped into the mouth and ran through the body and the young man cut off yet another head. "Hm," said *nïmïrïka,* "let's take another rest."

After about five minutes *nïmïrïka* said to the young man: "You're doing pretty well fighting, but I'm going to eat you up anyhow. Let's try it again." They got up and started scuffling again. Then fox, mink, and jackrabbit ran through the body as before and the young man cut off one more head. That left only three heads. "Well boy," said *nïmïrïka,* "let's take another rest." They rested for a short while. *Nïmïrïka* said, "Looks like he's got the best deal, I'm getting weak now. Well, I hope that I'll make it, I want to eat. Well, boy, let's try it again." They started again and once more fox, mink and jackrabbit ran through *nïmïrïka* cutting him as they ran, and the young man cut off yet another head.

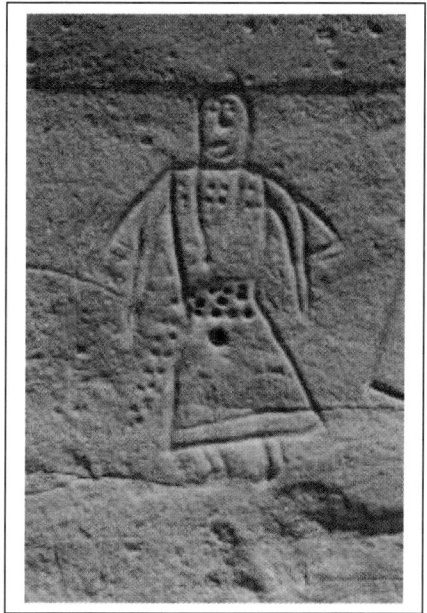

There were only two heads left now. "Hm," said *Pandzó:apits,* "let's have a little rest." The young girl was very happy that the young man was fighting so hard for her. "Well, my boy, said *Pandzó:apits*, "one of us is going to die pretty soon. Let's try it again." They got up and started fighting once more. Fox jumped into the mouth of *nïmïrïka.* He was followed by mink and jackrabbit, and when they came out at the rear end, the young man cut off another head. Now there was only one head left and that was the largest one. "Let's take a rest," said *nïmïrïka.*

"Now boy, I have to put up a good fight, this is the end. I have to do it."
Pandzó:apits did his best, but so did the young man, fox, mink and
jackrabbit. When jackrabbit came out of the rear end of *Pandzó:apits* for the
last time, the young man swung his sword and cut off the last head, and
Pandzó:apits fell dead down to the floor.

The King was amazed and said, "I wonder who this boy is who managed to
kill *Pandzó:apits*. My daughter's life has been saved, but he must show me
the seven tongues."

92

Now there was a coloured fellow there who had killed seven sheep and had taken out their tongues. There was also another man, who could have been either white or Indian, who had killed seven mules and had taken out their tongues. And one more man had killed seven hogs and also taken out their tongues. The King said, "My daughter gave a diamond ring to this boy, but I still want to find out who he is." The girl asked the three pets, "what would you like to eat for dinner?" Fox said, "I would like roast turkey." Mink said, "I would like roast chicken," and Jackrabbit said: "I would like sweet cookies." It was decided that a "trial" be held after dinner to find out who had killed the seven-headed *Pandzó:apits.*

All the four men who had the tongues were called in, the judges sat at the side of "the crown," and the girl was "on the stage." The young man who had killed *Pandzó:apits* had the tongues in his pocket. The coloured man walked to and fro and had the tongues in his belt. He had a rather arrogant look on his face and when he passed the judges they said: "No, these tongues don't look like *nïmïrïka's* tongues, they look like sheep tongues. The next man passed the judges, he was the one with the mule tongues. The judges said, "No, these tongues don't look like *nïmïrïka's* tongues, they look like mule tongues. Then it was the turn of the third man to pass the judges, he was the one with the hog's tongues. The judges said, "no, these tongues don't look like *nïmïrïka's* tongues, they look like hog's tongues."

Now it was the turn of the young man who really did have the tongues of the *nïmïrïka,* and his pets were with him. Jackrabbit said, "Too quick," before the judges had time to say anything: "we're the ones who killed the *nïmïrïka."* The girl immediately recognised the young man with his pets. Yellow Crown asked her: "Is this the boy who saved you?" "Yes, it is," answered the girl. "What about the other fellows who have tongues?" asked Yellow Crown. "No," said the girl, "they have no pets, but this boy has Fox, Mink and Jackrabbit."

The coloured fellow wanted to argue about it. "No," he said, "I am the man who killed the *nïmïrïka."* Then the King said: "take this liar out and burn him up!" They took him away and threw him in the fire. That is why blacks have such kinky hair, and why they are so black.
Jackrabbit said, "we're the men who killed the *nïmïrïka."* So he married the King's daughter. *Ušú:weye?* – that's the end. *Tïna páshaytazakogen* – it will be a good winter![6]

A *nïmïrïka*
"This story will keep boys at home, and prevent them from making noise!"

One family, consisting of father, mother, and their two sons and a grandfather (mother's father), split off from the large camp and went to camp on their own. They made their camp in the mountains where there were lots of game tracks. As soon as they had set up camp, the father and grandfather went off to hunt. They both returned late in the evening but the son-in-law arrived home earlier than the grandfather. The grandfather told them how he had seen the tracks of a *nïmïrïka* not very far from their camp. "You have to keep the boys quiet," he said. It was getting dark and one of the boys got mad because he couldn't find something that he was looking for.[7] They refused to find it for him and he started howling loudly. The father said, "Keep quiet boy you are making too much noise here." But he didn't say that the *nïmïrïka* was close by. The boy went on howling though and his father said again, "Hey, stop that noise!" They all went into the tipi where the mother was cooking some meat on the fire.

While she was busy cooking *nïmïrïka* entered the lodge and carrying a sack that looked like a cap. "Come here, my little grandson," he said. "I have got a nice, warm cap for you to wear, and I want to put it on you. We'll have to warm it first though, for it is cold inside." He warmed a sack over the fire, holding it with both his hands, [John demonstrated]. "Come here now grandson," said *nïmïrïka* "it is warm enough for you now." He put the sack on his head, and the boy jumped around shaking all over. Then he pulled the sack over the boy's head, and pulled it down. "That's what I want to do," he said. "That's what makes a good little boy." Then he grabbed the other boy, slapped him, and knocked him out. He put both the boys in the sack and said, "Now I have nice, tender meat, and I will go home and feed my little ones; this is good food for my kids." Then he walked away.

The boy that he had slapped came to, and saw through the sack that there was a branch of a tree hanging over the trail where *nïmïrïka* was walking. When *nïmïrïka* came close to the branch, the little boy managed to grab hold of it and pull himself out of the sack. Luckily *nïmïrïka* didn't notice that the boy had escaped. The boy hung there onto the branch until *nïmïrïka* had lumbered away, then he jumped down from the branch, and ran home back to the camp. His father and mother were very glad to see him, and so was the grandfather. But the other boy never returned.

Two stories told to Åke Hultkrantz by the Medicine Man, George Wesaw

A long time ago Jackson Hole was a place where the Indians used to wander around the forest and ride along the creeks; there were flowers all around and the water was soft and calm. One day an Indian left his camp and arrived at this idyllic place. He really liked it there and he stayed until evening. He prepared for his homeward journey, but it had become dark and although the stars were shining, there was no moon. He was on foot and he came to a cliff. It started to rain and got cold. Suddenly he felt warm air in front of him and so he walked towards it and found that it was coming from a cave where there was a fire. It seemed to be the home of somebody and he saw a man sitting inside the cave. It was a *nïmïrïka*. He said to the Indian, "You can come in and rest awhile if you like, but then we shall have a fight." After a short rest they had a fight and fought hard; they tumbled around and became exhausted but the Indian managed to throw off the *nïmïrïka*, who then said, "Alright, you win!" Because he had won the *nïmïrïka* bestowed on him a special power or medicine and said to him, "Whoever tries to kill you will not succeed." The Indian stayed there all night and left in the morning. If the *nïmïrïka* had won he would have eaten up the Indian. George Wesaw finished by saying, "That's the end of the story, but it's a true story!"

This took place a long, long time ago. A group of Indians decided to make camp for the night, and they divided themselves up into two camps three to four miles apart from each other. During the night there was a severe snowstorm and the next morning the snow was between six to seven feet deep. Even though the camps were quite a distance from each other they could still see the smoke from the other camp.

One morning, one of the groups didn't see any smoke coming from the other camp and they sent one of their men to see what had happened. When he arrived he found all the tipis empty, but there was a *wútєyga* – (brush house) close by and smoke was coming from it. He looked around carefully and then entered. What did he see but a twelve year old crippled boy lying down chewing on a human skull. There had been four or five other men there but they were out hunting. The Indian who looked into the brush house was really terrified at what he saw and ran back to his camp to tell them all. The Chief called all the warriors together and they went off to attack the cannibals – *nïmïrïkas*. By the time they reached the camp the hunters were sleeping. The warriors set fire to the brush. The *nïmïrïkas* rushed out, and they were attacked and killed.

History of the *ninïmbïs*- pygmies
(told from one generation to the next)

John Trehero had heard about the pygmies from his grandmother. Although she had never seen any herself, she knew of them as a race that had existed long, long ago. John called them small *tukurika,* or he even preferred the term *t eitïdzi: tóyai* – little mountain people.

John also told about the white men who were prospecting for uranium up in the Dinwoody area when they saw two small fellows going down to the water with baskets. The little people then went up to the rocks and disappeared. The white men didn't know where they were. They saw them every day for about a week, and tried to catch them. But the little people always went down to the water in different places, so it was impossible to know which way they would go. Consequently the white guys couldn't manage to take a picture of them. The whites also tried to follow them up into the rocks but they could not find them!

These little people existed all over the Rocky Mountains, right up to Canada; and, said John "they might have been here in the Wind River Mountains." However, there is no archaeological evidence of them and they are no longer to be seen. The Indians in the Wind River area now believe that these little people went north and are today the same as the Eskimo in Alaska. These little people were about the same height as four year olds, but they were built proportionally and had well-developed muscles. They spoke the Shoshone language and they lived on pine nuts, mutton and fish. Their clothes were made from mountain sheep fur, and their dwellings were caves in the rocks. They had no horses, and they were not nomads like the great *tukurika,* "but," said John "they could travel long distances on skis, each one with a sheep on his back[8]."

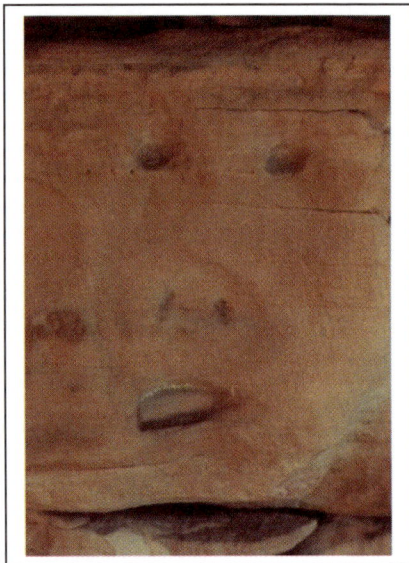

Story about a Witch,
Told by Enge Shoyo, (son of Polly Shoyo, a renowned story-teller born around 1878)

There were two brothers who lived in a home made of sagebrush. They had bows and made their arrows out of bone and kept them carefully. One day the older of the two decided that they should go hunting. The older brother said: "we are going to travel through dangerous places and whatever I say, you must follow my advice." The younger one, who usually liked to go his own way and do as he always wanted, finally agreed to do as he was told.

They left to hunt, and the older brother warned that the danger was their aunts! The younger brother couldn't understand that. "Are our aunts dangerous?" he asked. But as he didn't get any answer they carried on their way. Ahead of them, although a long way away they saw the aunts playing. They were throwing each other up in the air. The older brother said, "Don't go up there, they can throw you up in the air and break your neck." The younger brother couldn't make it out. "Are they the ones who would throw us in the air and kill us," he asked wonderingly. His brother said, "Don't go there!" But the younger one said, "I want to go there." "Can't you take my advice," said the older brother. "No," said his brother and he went over to the aunts, leaned against a pine tree and watched them. The aunts noticed him and said: "there is our nephew over there; he has come to visit us." *Püppöranzogupä* – Weasel, was the name of the younger brother, and the aunts said to him, "why don't you try this game and see how good you will feel?" He did as they asked and they jerked him harder and harder each time he came down and he really got hurt. Then he said, "Take it easy," but they just carried on as before so that Weasel started jerking them. The women said, "Don't jerk us too hard"; but three times when they came down *Püppöranzogupä* jerked them very hard. They flew so high that when they came down they hit themselves so hard they died.

Now he saw that they were really bears. He cut up the largest one, the mother-bear, skinned her and then went into the nostrils. He took some of the blood, put it all over the bear head and then crept back into the nose. The older brother had meanwhile gone off, but Weasel followed him, jumped up two or three times and acted like a bear, so that he soon caught up with his brother. The older brother looked around twice and then said: "it's bad that *Püppöranzogupä* didn't follow my advice, I expect that he has been killed by now." Then he hid himself. After having circled around a couple of times, he prepared his bow. Weasel came hopping along, stopped, and then the older brother shot him near his shoulder. Weasel just crawled out of the nose. When the older brother saw Weasel he said, "I could have easily killed you." But *Püppöranzogupä* said, "Yes, but I am too clever for you to kill me!"

They carried on their journey. Then the older brother said, "do you see up there, there is a cliff, and it is a very dangerous place." Weasel said, "I want to go up and have a look at it." His older brother said, "At the top of that cliff is your aunt, and she is going to fool you and make you jump into the water. There is a lot of water up there and she lives there. She is a *pánzóaváipö* – witch. "Is she so bad that she tricks people and kills them?" asked Weasel. This wasn't enough to put *Püppöranzogupä* off, and after an argument just like the other time, he decided not to take his brother's advice. He ran up the cliff to the place where the witch was supposed to be.

She was there and was talking loudly saying, "There is a buck mountain sheep standing down there." She repeated this again and again and Weasel crept up behind her and said, "What are you talking about?" The witch swung round and saw Weasel and said, "Oh, is it you my nephew, standing here?" And then she said, "Look down at the buck mountain sheep over there." *Püppöranzogupä* looked down at where she had pointed and she pushed him slightly. *Püppöranzogupä* said, "kisch, kisch, kisch, wait a minute. The witch stopped and *Püppöranzogupä* said, "What is it?" She replied, "Look further down there!" *Püppöranzogupä* looked down and she gave him a hefty push, but he had understood what she was going to do. He hopped round the cliff, crept up behind her and pushed her over so that the fall killed her.

Püppöranzogupä ran back to where his brother was and said, "I killed that lady over there although she thought that she was cunning enough to kill people. She tried to push me off the cliff but I ran around the rock and pushed her off instead. That is why I am standing here before you now." The older brother said, "Is it really you *Püppöranzogupä?* Do you mean to tell me that you have killed the witch?" "Yes," replied *Püppöranzogupä,* "and I guess that I have in fact killed my aunt."

They carried on their way and the older brother said, "Now lets try some more hunting and it can be very dangerous. I don't want to scare you *Püppöranzogupä. "* "I won't be scared," replied Weasel. "Let us go on to the ocean now." They went on their way and eventually they came to the ocean. The older brother once again said that he was worried that Weasel would be scared when things became dangerous, but Weasel just said once more, "I won't be scared." The older brother told Weasel to wait for him on the shore, then went into the water where there was a water elk. He stood deep in the water so that only his shoulders and head were above the water surface. He grabbed the water elk and they started to fight. They both disappeared under the water three times. Meanwhile *Püppöranzogupä* saw what was happening and got tired of waiting. He even thought that his brother might die, so he shot an arrow towards the ripples on the water. He got scared, though, at what he might have done, So he ran away.

Meanwhile the older brother managed to kill the water elk, and he pulled it towards the shore, cut it up, looked around, but couldn't see his younger brother anywhere. Just then two muskrats, *pámpuqáno* appeared. They raced round in circles on the surface on the water, and when they came to the place where the older brother was the sun had risen and the day had dawned. They were uncles of the brothers. The older brother said, "Your nephew, Weasel, got scared and ran away. I don't know where he went. Perhaps he is very hungry by now. Would you please find him wherever he is, and give him a piece of this elk meat, as well as some elk punch (that was made from the stomach of the elk), and some water in case he needs it. Please find him, and say that this meat is from the elk that his older brother shot. If you find him unconscious you have to use some dried, wild rose brush with thorns, and stick it in his aha hole, push it backwards and forwards until the yellow aha comes out. That is the only way to revive him.

The muskrats went off and eventually found Weasel, *püppöranzogupä,* who was unconscious. They used twigs from the rose brush just as they had been told to do, and weasel woke up. "Oh, uncles," he said joyfully, and gave them both a hug. Then the muskrats handed over the things that they had brought with them and said, "Your brother has sent these things for you." Weasel laughed and said, "So this is what my brother has shot." Then he ate and drank until he was quite satisfied, left his two uncles, and went on his way to return to his brother. The two muskrats went back to the water and swam off.

Weasel finally arrived at the place where his older brother was and they built a fire and ate and drank. As the night fell and it grew darker and darker the older brother said, "This is really a dangerous place and we better not have a fire tonight and eat at the same time." Weasel said, "is it really dangerous brother, is it really so dangerous? His older brother replied, "Tomorrow we can eat," and Weasel repeated: "tomorrow we can eat, this is a dangerous place." The older brother became irritated as Weasel repeated everything he said, but he said once more to Weasel, "this is a dangerous place, we cannot build a fire here, something will come and take us away! "The *wokaimunbitsch* – monster-like bird, can see the fire however far away it is, and will come and get us." Then they lay down to sleep. *Püppöranzogupä* the weasel said, "Is it really true that *wokaimunbitsch* will take us away? But there was no answer. They slept for about two hours when Weasel said again, "Oh, brother, I am so hungry, can't I have something to eat?" "No," said his brother, you can't have anything to eat at night. It is too dangerous; the *wokaimunbitsch* will come and take you away."

They lay down and went to sleep again, but after a while Weasel asked the same question again. His brother answered in the same way as before. This occurred four times, and in the end the older brother was so irritated that he said, "Well, Weasel, go ahead and build a fire and eat some food." Weasel lit a fire and cooked some food. Meanwhile his older brother got up, walked 50 – 100 yards, lay down and listened and waited. Weasel sat by the fire, and ate. Suddenly the older brother felt something fly by and muttered to himself, "there he comes, that *wokaimunbitch,* my silly brother will now be taken by him."

The swishing noise increased and soon was a storm wind, which blew out the fire. However, Weasel didn't seem to take any notice and went on eating. He said to his older brother, "wouldn't you like something to eat?" There was no answer. Again he said, "Wouldn't you like some of this food?" and he passed over some food. The *wokaimunbitch* just looked at him with his claws pointing at him. Weasel looked surprised and said, "What do you want, why have you come here?" He repeated his question when he didn't get any reply. Then he took up an elk bone and offered it to the *wokaimunbitch* saying, "Maybe you would like this bone (although all the flesh had been eaten off the bone). He then threw the bone at the bird, and knocked him down! "Look brother," he said, "I have knocked him down!" But his brother didn't hear him because he was hiding far away.

Weasel went on eating and the *wokaimunbitch* recovered and touched the bone! Then the *wokaimunbitch* tried to take Weasel. But Weasel moved away and said, "Hey, brother, you missed me!" The *wokaimunbitch* tried to grab Weasel twice, but he missed, and Weasel said again, "brother, you missed me!" The *wokaimunbitch* tried three more times to grab Weasel but he was unsuccessful, and Weasel said gleefully, "ha, you missed me again!" But on the fourth attempt the *wokaimunbitsch* managed to grab Weasel's private parts – *vŭ,* with his claws. Weasel shrieked "Oh brother, this *wokaimunbitch* has got hold of my *vŭ,* I guess that he will take me away now! Oh, he is taking me away!" And that is just what *wokaimunbitch* did. The older brother had heard all this and thought to himself, "This is just what I thought. If that stupid brother had followed my advice, this would not have happened to him."

The *wokaimunbitch* flew away with Weasel to an island where an old woman lived, and she said to Weasel, "That *wokaimunbitch* brought me here many, many years ago when I was a young girl. There are many skeletons lying all over the island, and they are what remain of the animals that *wokaimunbitch* has brought here and then eaten up. Now he has brought you here and there is no way out, you will have to stay here." Then she asked Weasel, "Have you any ideas as to how we can get rid of *wokaimunbitch?* He didn't say anything so she went on, "I guess that if you can find a sharp flint stone; we can then split it up into small pieces and perhaps I can make a stew out of it that he can eat.

Püppöranzogupä went off and returned a little later with a sharp piece of flint stone. Meanwhile the *wokaimunbitch* was out hunting some new prey. The old woman mixed the pieces of flint into the stew and when the *wokaimunbitch* returned she let him eat as much as he liked of it as he was very hungry. After he had eaten he couldn't move and said that he felt sick and he shook all over. After shaking a while he fell backwards on to his back and died. And that's how they killed him!

The old woman then said, "And how shall you get back home again? I see that the wing span of the *wokaimunbitch* is ten feet long, perhaps we can make a canoe from them. They worked hard for several days and then the canoe was finished. The old woman then told Weasel to go and collect firewood. "Take sagebrush," she said, "for that burns on the water. Weasel collected the sagebrush. He now had enough firewood to last him on his journey over the ocean. Before he left the old woman said, "be careful, it's dangerous on the water and all sorts of water animals – *nynymussi,* will try to get into the canoe. I won't be coming with you as I am so old and want to stay and die here. Now that the *wokaimunbitch* is dead, you can light a fire at night without feeling afraid. I shall watch you as long as I can see you before you disappear over the horizon.

Püppöranzogupä, Weasel paddled his wood paddle hard; soon the night fell and he had only managed to paddle a quarter of a mile from the old woman! The second night he found himself in the same place! On the third night he had only gone forward a small distance. He must have been further away but at sea it didn't look so far.

On the fourth night the old woman could see him a little, but not much. But he was further away. Then on the fifth night he seemed much further away although she could slightly see the fire that he had made in the canoe. On the sixth night he was a bit further away and on the seventh night the old woman saw the fire very faintly. Then on the eighth night he seemed a good deal further away, and on the ninth night she could hardly see any light from the fire. When she looked on the tenth night she couldn't see any light at all. Weasel had now disappeared from sight. We don't know how far or how long he paddled, but the two muskrats were making their rounds when they saw their nephew in the canoe. They pulled the canoe towards land and helped him ashore. Weasel was so glad to see them and gave them both a big hug! Today the two muskrats are water spirits and are still living in the water.

The younger brother, *Püppöranzogupä* went off to the mountains where he still lives. But the older brother, who became a human, went off to the southwest to seek out an Indian tribe, so that he could join them. He was on his way when darkness fell, and he arrived at a very spooky place, where several human beings were throwing stones around. He stood quite still and then heard a mysterious noise that came closer. A strange creature approached and looked at him and said, "It looks as if he is a human, he has hands, eyes, mouth etc." The older brother didn't dare to move, but in the morning he felt quite normal again and could continue his wandering. The whole day he went on, and then in the evening when it became very dark he heard a screech owl howling, and with every howl it flashed out lightening. The older brother ran as fast as he could until he came to a wide river, which he jumped when one of the flashes of lightening appeared.

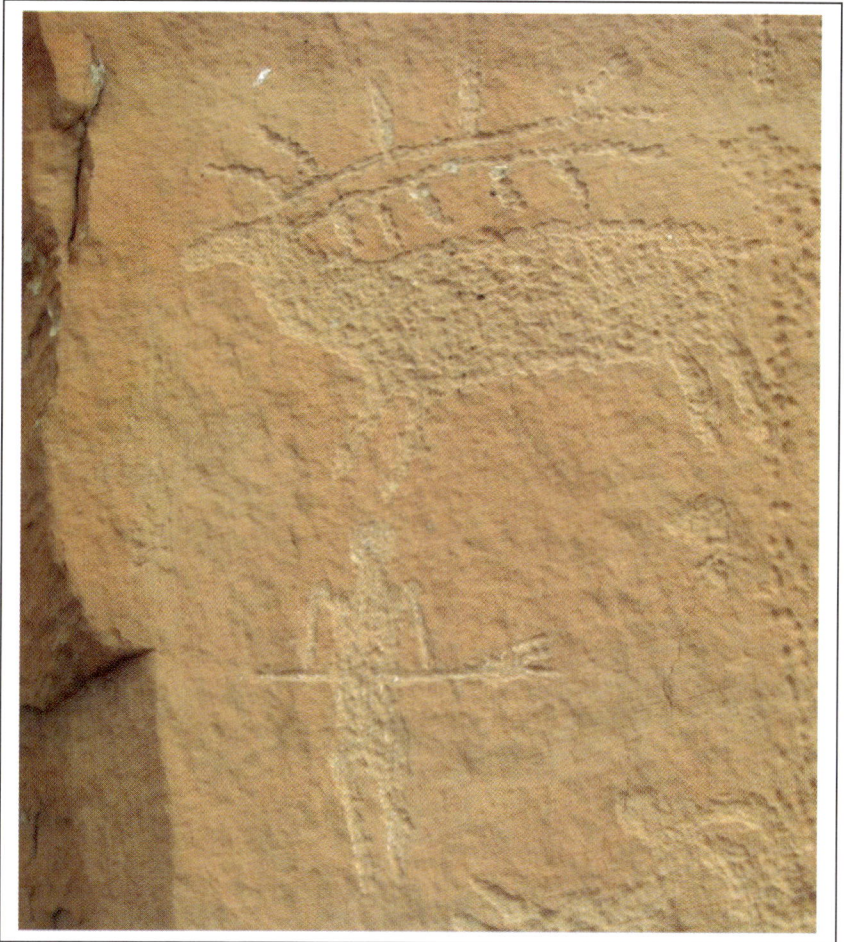

In the morning he went off wandering again, and went on the whole day until once more the darkness fell. He entered the woods, and heard a noise. He stood still as something making a thumping noise grew closer and closer. Somebody hit the tree where he was standing, but luckily it missed him and went on its way. Once more the dawn came and he carried on.

He came upon an idea. He covered his legs with leaves and twigs and carried on like that with his wandering. Then he came to a place with masses and masses of rattlesnakes. They bit him again and again but at last he managed to get out of that place.

The night fell and he rested. The next morning he carried on once more and came to a whole field of cactus! He thought very hard and managed to convince himself that he could make it. He went through the cactus field, even though his feet got covered in thorns, but he still carried on. When night fell he saw an enormous fire in front of him; he stopped, looked at the fire, and went on. He stood still again when he came to a dark place and could just make out people moving around without making a sound.

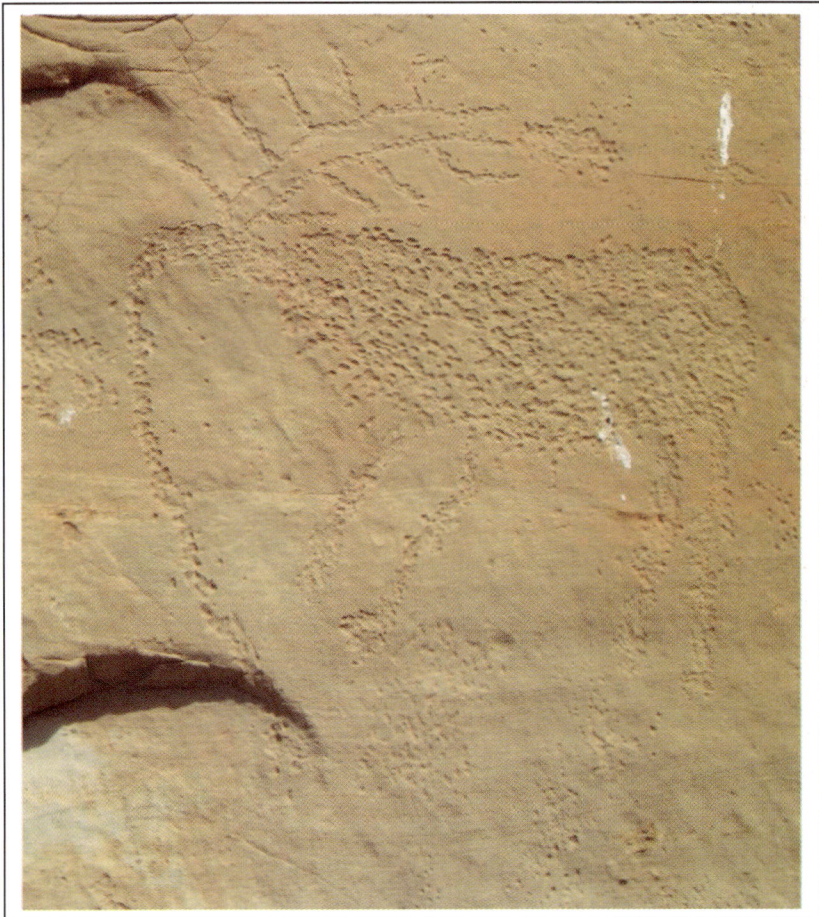

He saw that elk meat had been cut up, which the people were cooking over the fire. But when they smelt the meat they threw it away. There were two people sitting apart from the others and *Püppöranzogupä*'s brother went over to them, sat down beside them, and just watched them. When they discovered him, they talked to him in their way, sort of gesturing as they were silent because they had no mouths. But very kindly, they offered him some food. The older brother accepted the food and swallowed it. Then one of them gestured to him to please cut an opening for his mouth! So the brother did as he was asked and cut open an opening for a mouth. Voice sounds came out of the newly cut mouth and the man began to eat. He managed to both talk and eat at the same time! When all the other people saw what the older brother had done, they all went over to him and he did the same for them. It was in this way that human beings got their mouths. That's the end of it, that's the way it happened!

Notes

1. Åke Hultkrantz remarked that George Wesaw had told him that there were dragons in Washakie Hot Springs, but Deborah Trehero characterised George Wesaw as being "bad".
2. **Deborah intervened and told John that two of their granddaughters had spent a night in a** cave at Thermopolis Hot Springs. She said they didn't dream anything during the night.
3. John mentioned here that in earlier days the *nïmïrïka* lived all around there, both in the mountains and on the prairie. "Elephants were *nïmïrïka* some time ago, they say."
4. "Usually," said John Trehero, "Rock Hide is 12 feet tall and weighs 500 pounds or more. He looks like a human, but has tough skin."
5. John commented, "This weakened the *nïmïrïka.*"
6. When this story was told it aroused laughter: for example when the animals ran out of the rear end of the *nïmïrïka;* when jackrabbit says that the three pets actually did the deed, and also when the explanation was given of how the black men became so black.
7. The thing that he was looking for was probably his cap, as it figures later on in the story.
8. John Trehero also maintained that the great *tukurika* also used skis and bows made from the horns of mountain sheep.

Chapter 6

Practical Jokes: Competitions between Medicine Men to see who had the strongest *puha*
Dangerous Spirits – but also helping Spirits

Joking relationships exist between a man and his brother's wife (sister-in-law), as well as her sister. In the same way a woman can have a joking relationship with her husband's brother (brother-in-law). [Please note though that a man's brother's wife is called "wife," and a woman's husband's brother is called her husband.]

A Joking Story

A man was married to the older of two sisters, but he was not satisfied with her. When the younger sister's husband died, he said to his brother-in-law, the brother of his wife, "I want to marry your other sister. I don't want the woman I have; she's mean with me all the time." His brother-in-law answered: "I don't like to break up my sister's home." The man wasn't happy with the reply that he got and said, "If you talk to your sister on my behalf, I will give you my best horse. I'll treat you all as before, but I prefer your youngest sister." "Well," said his brother-in-law, who really didn't like the whole idea, "I'll think about it, but I don't want to destroy my sister's home for the sake of a horse." "No," said the man, "You talk for me."

The brother-in-law went to his older sister's home and told her what her husband had said, and she said: "Well, we can fix him. I'll talk to my younger sister and we'll play a joke on him. We can have a dance."
The brother went to his older sister's husband and said: "Now, brother-in-law, my younger sister has agreed to go with you if you are willing to go take her to another tribe. Otherwise if you stay here, her older sister will fight with her." Yes," said the man, "I will agree to that. We can live with another tribe for two or three years and then we can return here." "Alright," said the brother-in-law, we are going to have a dance and she will leave with you after the dance."

After the dance the man went outside to look for her and found her out in the dark. They went off together and when it was almost daylight they left the trail and made camp. The man said, "I don't like your sister and I'll tell you why," and then he started talking. He went on and on so much that he put himself to sleep! When he woke up later on the next day and looked around he saw that the woman with him was his old wife! This really made him mad and he said: "I'll whip my brother-in-law! He made me sleep with my own wife!"

106

A Joke told by Charlie Washakie

Once upon a time a man, a stranger, was travelling around. Way out in the desert he met a man on horseback who stopped and asked him where he was going. "I am on my way to the place where the king lives, to ask him for something to live on," replied the tramp. The rider said, "I understand that you are a man who is full of tricks." "Oh, no," said the tramp, "I do not think that I am going to play any tricks today, I am too nervous. I left all my jokes up in the mountains, way over there where you can see the pine trees in the distance." "Well," said the rider, "I can lend you my horse if you go up there to fetch your jokes." The man thought for a while and replied, "Ah, yes, I could do that if you'd like me to." "Right," said the man with the horse. "Just you do that and then come back here again."

The joker mounted the horse and rode off. Soon afterwards though the horse bucked the rider off and went back to his owner. "What's the matter with that horse!" exclaimed the joker when he had arrived back at where he had started from on the horse. "He wants you to have my boots," said the man, and took off his boots and handed them over to the joker. The joker put them on, climbed back on the horse and started off again. But as soon as he had gone a little way the horse bucked him off again. Once more the horse went back to his owner and the tramp followed. "What is the matter with your horse?" he asked. The other man replied, "He wants you to have my spurs."

The joker put on the spurs, climbed back on the horse and rode off. This time he managed to get a little further before the horse threw him off.

When he arrived back at the starting point once again the owner of the horse said to him, "He wants you to have my pants." The joker put on the pants and started off again. But he was again kicked off. This time the man said "Put on my shirt." The joker put the shirt on and started off again. It didn't help though, and as soon as he had got a little on his way the horse bucked him once more. "He wants you to have my hat too," said the owner of the horse. So the joker put the hat on and rode off. "That's it," he said "You can walk now and I will ride home!" "Oh, said the owner of the horse and clothes, "So the joke's on me!"

Competitions between Medicine Men
to see who had the strongest *Puha* (power)

Concerning the control of *puha:* if someone said that he had received a vision from his *puha* (spirit), then he had to prove it. For example if an older medicine man wanted him as his assistant then he had three days to show that he could get a sick person on his feet again. Many medicine men demonstrated their power by having competitions. Here follows two accounts of such competitions:[1]

A true story (according to John Trehero) from the middle of the 1800's:

There were a couple of old fellows sitting on a woodpile bragging about their *puha. Ayguidá?* ("Long Horns"), said "Well, *Yú:rïka* ('Grease Eater'), I want you to show me something first so that you can prove to me that you have *puha."* *Yú:rïka* said *"Alright Ayguidá?"* I shall show you something, what would you like me to do?" "Well," said *Yú:rïka,* "when I have done my stuff I want you to prove yours." "Very well," replied *Ayguidá?*

A magpie came along just then and went up close to them. "Now *Ayguidá?,"* said *Yú:rïka,* "I'll show you a trick here. Watch pretty close." *Yú:rïka,* blew on his fist [John Trehero demonstrated], and then the magpie jumped around and fell down dead. "Well," *Ayguidá?,* said, "that's very wonderful; you could save men going to be killed by outlaws. It is a pretty powerful *puha* you have." "Now," said *Yú:rïka,* "it is time for you to show me your *puha.*" "Alright," replied *Ayguidá?,* "now watch that man coming along the road. When I blow, we'll see what happens to him. But I won't kill him." A man was riding along the road and *Ayguidá?* blew on his fist [once again John demonstrated], and the horse started bucking the fellow and threw him off.

"What did you do to that horse?" *Yú:rïka* asked. "Well," *Ayguidá? s*aid, "I blew on my fist, and my *puha* threw that fellow off!" [Please note here that as John demonstrated what had happened, he blew on his clenched fist through the hole that had been formed by the fingers.]

Pandzïtá:ygö ("Bare Spot") and *Kïvoraipi:vo* ("Long Belly"), were working on a government ditch using teams of horses. *Pandzïtá:ygö* said to *Kïvoraipi:vo,* "Hey, Long Belly, I want you to prove something that I have heard about you. Can you do some tricks?" "Yes," said *Kïvoraipi:vo,* "if you are willing to put up some money, I will do a trick." "Oh," *Pandzïtá:ygö* said, "that's my kind of deal, because I have some tricks that I can do too." ["That liar," laughed John.] "Alright *Pandzïtá:ygö,* " said *Kïvoraipi:vo,* " I have got $3.80 cents. If you can play a better trick than I can, you win. But if I can play a better trick then I win. Tricks when we quit work at noon."

When noon came *Kïvoraipi:vo* said, "*Pandzïtá:ygö,* you pull your trick out first." There were some other boys around, and they said. "Hey, wait you guys, we want to put up some money too. We bet that *Kïvoraipi:vo* will win, he has a pretty good trick." *Pandzïtá:ygö* asked *Kïvoraipi:vo,* "Do you want me to put up my trick first?" "Yes," said *Kïvoraipi:vo,* "and here is the money." "Alright *Kïvoraipi:vo,* I'll show you. The horses of the first plow team that comes over that hill will run away out of control." "What's your trick *Kïvoraipi:vo?* " "I'll do mine right here," said *Kïvoraipi:vo. "*Do you see that tent over there?" "Yes, I do." "Well, when I blow in my hand, that tent will fall down." *Pandzïtá:ygö,* said, "there's no plow team in sight yet, but you go ahead and blow down that tent."

Kïvoraipi:vo held up his hand, blew on it, and the wind blew down the tent. *Pandzïtá:ygö* said, "you can't call that a trick, what do you call it? You are a *tú:kuyuiki* (magician).[2] But I am going to do a real trick." *Kïvoraipi:vo* said,

"You are going to do a *tú:kuyuiki* too, if those horses run away from that fellow." They waited for ten to fifteen minutes, then a plow team appeared with four horses. All at once the horses seemed to get scared of something; they started running faster and faster and the workers jumped off. But *Kïvoraipi:vo* won, for he had just blown and showed his power first.

"Alright," said *Pandzïtá:ygö*, "tomorrow at noon we'll have another contest." "No," said *Kïvoraipi:vo*, "let's do it right now; we have time." *Pandzïtá:ygö* said, "I only have $1.50 cents! You pull off your trick first *Kïvoraipi:vo.*" *Kïvoraipi:vo* went over and got hold of a short rope. Then he laid it out towards *Pandzïtá:ygö's* horse. "Well," said *Kïvoraipi:vo*, "when I jerk this rope we will see *Pandzïtá:ygö's* horse jump around, acting crazy." He jerked on the rope, but the horse did not get scared. "Well," said *Kïvoraipi:vo*, "you made out pretty well the first time, but not now, and I am the winner again!"

Dangerous Spirits
The Fish Woman

Peywiwaipö ("fish-woman") is a water spirit, said to be an "evil spirit." You cannot pray to her for good luck in fishing and she cannot control the fishes. She is not identical with the water-woman who resembles a baby. The fish-woman is of a "regular human size." From her waist she has a fish tail, but she is human from the waist upwards, although she is covered in fish scales. She has long, brown hair that reaches down to her knees. Here are three accounts:

1. A long time ago at the Dinwoody Lakes, where there is a ranch nowadays, people used to see her when they moved camp. They tried to catch her but she always managed to disappear.
2. She has been seen at Bull Lake. Two Shoshoni half-breeds saw her lying on the sand at the shore. But they said that she crawled back into the water when she saw them.
3. (Untrue story according to John Trehero): *Pandzïtá:ygö* was at Fort Washakie and had a visit from the fish-woman, who wanted him. She had travelled up from Bull Lake all the way along the Wind River to Riverton and from there along the Little Wind River to the Fort. *Pandzïta:ygö* told her to go home again and that he would marry her during the coming spring. So she took the same long way back, dived in the water at Bull Lake and disappeared.

Ghosts – *dzó:ap*

Ghosts or apparitions are spirits with tails that have straight horns pointing upwards,[3] thin long faces and finger nails as long as cat claws. They are black. John Trehero denied that masks had been used to represent the faces of the ghosts. Five people had seen them near the Bar that was situated in Fort Washakie between John and Deborah's home and the churchyard. John said that he had never actually seen a ghost. However, close to the Bar a man called Jim Compton, [the son of one of Åke Hultkrantz's interpreters], and his wife said that they had seen some ghosts. They were sitting in their car, drinking beer after sunset, when two ghosts appeared in the backseat of their car and whispered in their ears, "Hey, will you take us home?" Jim and his wife didn't answer and the ghosts disappeared!

One evening an Arapaho and his wife had just been released from jail and were walking along the road towards Ethete. A car came up behind them, and they stepped to the side of the road to allow it to pass. The car slowed down and pulled in to where they were standing. The man who was driving asked, "Would you like a little ride to wherever you are going?" "Oh, yes, thank you," they replied, and climbed into the car. It drove off. The woman looked around uncomfortably and said. "I want to get out; do you notice that man?" "Don't be afraid," said her husband, "he is our friend." But she insisted that she wanted to get out of the car. The driver stopped the car when they got to Charlie Redman's house. The Arapaho and his wife climbed out of the car and the car drove off. The lights of the car disappeared and then the whole car just disappeared into thin air! The wife had seen that the driver had horns and very bright eyes just like a ghost, and that was why she was so frightened, but her husband hadn't noticed what the driver had looked like.

The Spirits in the Mountains

Pandzïtá:ygö stated that there were spirits in the mountain at Bull Lake. They opened a door in the mountain and asked him to go inside. There they were playing a handgame and he sat down beside a girl who wanted to give him handgame *puha,* power. However he didn't want to receive that as he would have had to touch her bones, and that made him think about his own bones, so he refused.

Holy Mountains and Sacrificial Stones

John Trehero said that there was a rocky point in the mountains that you had to pass around to be safe. People should not go there unless they had something to give. If you passed without making a sacrifice you would have very bad luck. This mountain is called *Šïkigare* – "Black Butte," and is situated between two high peaks close to Pinedale. There is very "evil *puha*" there.

Long ago at Pryor Gap there was a rock where arrows, meat hides etc. were offered, but mostly arrows. That was said to give the one who offered the arrows better luck when hunting. Many people took off their moccasins when they passed by that rock. The rock was more the house of *puha* rather than *puha* itself.

The Magic of the Evil Eye

This magic is called *tukuyui:?iki,[4]* meaning "you shocked him with your nerve," or "he got a shot from another person." When someone looks at you with **the evil eye,** it makes you "feel as though your food has got stuck in you half way down, you can't manage to get it down." A person who has **the evil eye** knows that he or she has it: when you feel your eyes blink, "that's when the poison hits you." And if someone is eating and they look at him, they can shoot him with the **evil eye** which can "poison him."

The Legend of a Visit to the Realm of the Dead

A long, long time ago there were four Indians who were travelling across a large desert. They came to a mountain but they could not go over the mountain although they were travelling on foot. There was a cooley there and they saw many tracks leading to a hole in the mountain. "I guess this is a tunnel through the mountain," said one of them. They decided to go into the hole. "Well, I don't see any light at the end of this tunnel yet," said another of them. Their chief said, "We'll just keep on going and see where it leads."

They went on and on. After a while one of them said, "Haven't we been travelling all day now, and still we don't see any sign of the sun." As they thought that it must be evening, they decided to stop and make camp, although they had nothing to eat. The chief laid a stick on the ground with its sharp end pointing in the direction that they were going. They took off their moccasins and lay down to go to sleep.

After a while one of them woke up and said, "Hey, boys, it looks to me as if it is morning. Let's go." They picked up the cane and followed the direction that it was pointing to, and walked and walked and walked. They travelled for a long time. Finally ahead of them they saw a ray of light, just about the size of a thumb nail. "Well, it looks like an outlet," said one of them. The light became brighter as they were walking and pretty soon they came close to the opening. When they actually went outside their vision was faint, they thought that it was due to the fact that they had been walking in the dark too long. They looked out and saw a stream where cottonwood was growing. "Well, boys, we had better go down and drink some water," said one of them.

They went down and there were a great many trees, like a forest. When they arrived they saw many camps, but they couldn't see any people. It looked quite deserted. They went over to a tipi and looked inside and found that everyone was asleep in there; in fact everyone in the whole camp seemed to be asleep. "Say," one of the four whispered, "these folks are sleeping; they must have the habit of sleeping in the daytime and not at night." Another of the four then said, "I wonder what is in that rawhide bag over there?" He untied the string and saw that there was a lot of dried meat in the bag. "See if there is any water in that jug," he said to the other fellow. "Yes," replied that man, "there is lots of water." They took the stuff outside and started to eat the dried meat and drink the water.

Round about sundown one of the men who had been sleeping came out of his tipi, looked at the four men and said, "Hey, you fellows have got up too early. We sleep in the daytime here in this country, and run around at night.

Have you got anything to eat?" "Yes," they said, "we have meat and water." "You need something more," said the newly-awakened man. "I have an axe here. Come in, my wife has got a fire made and she will cook for us. Where do you come from?" "We don't know," said the travellers. "We have no name for our country." "How did you get here?" asked the man. "We came right through the tunnel," replied the four travellers. "Oh, I see where you came from," said the man. "Don't go too far out of camp, you might get lost, and then you will have to stay here."

They had by now eaten a pretty good supper, although it was breakfast in that country. "Let's go and sleep now," said the chief of the four travellers. "Why don't we stay up like the people do here?" said one of the four. "No," said the chief, "it might not be good for us; we should stick to how we live in our own country." They made beds under a tree outside the camp and became very drowsy.

They heard the people in the village beat their drums and start to dance. One of the four men said, "Let me go and see." "No," said the chief, "we may not be doing the right thing here; let us stay here and see what rules there are in this country." They stayed in their beds, but at daybreak one of the nighthawks came over. "Hey," he said, "what are you doing here now? Everybody is going to sleep and you should not be out here." The chief said to his men, "I will tell you what is the best thing to do. Let's get a canteen full of water and a rawhide bag full of meat, and each one of us should make a torch by tying some sagebrush to a stick and putting some grease on it, and then we can walk back home through the tunnel." "No," said one of the men. "I don't think that one bag of meat will last long, we need more than that." But the chief replied. "We can't go out and steal food." "Well," said one of his men, "these people have plenty of food, and they are at home, we are not."

So each one of the four went out and found double rations. "That should last for the journey home," they said. The chief said, "It will take one day and one night to pass through the tunnel."

They left the camp and entered the tunnel again before noon that day, but they waited to light their torches. The tunnel was full of dirt and manure from buffaloes and other animals that travelled back and forth through the tunnel. The travellers kept on walking and it got darker and darker, and finally one of them lit his torch. They still kept going though until the chief said, "Well, I guess that it is about noon now. Let's stop to eat and drink." Now they couldn't see any sunlight but they started again as soon as they had eaten and kept going for quite a long time. They did not meet any animals. They went on walking until they all became very tired. One of the men said, "Let's stop here and eat again, then we can go on walking," So once more they ate, drank and then had a little sleep. Now it just happened that it was exactly the same spot where they had stopped to sleep on their way through the tunnel in the other direction. So, before they went to sleep they pointed the cane towards the way home.

When they thought that it was morning they started talking again. "I think that it must be morning now," said the chief. "Now, wash your hands, but don't use too much water." They all washed their hands, ate some breakfast, picked up the cane and started travelling again in the direction of home. They walked and walked and the tunnel seemed to get wider and it was cooler now. They thought that it must be about the middle of the afternoon. The chief said, "Now, brothers, remember that we have seen strange people that we have never seen before and our own people will probably never see."

They kept on walking, talking to each other at the same time and finally they saw a very small spot of light in the distance. They became excited when they understood that they were now pretty close to the opening. "Well boys," said the chief, "as soon as we get outside we will have a little food again. Then we can go back to our own country and tell our people our story. There are four of us who have seen what we have seen, so we have proof that we have been there." "What was the name of that place?" asked one of the men. "I don't know," answered the chief, "but we will call it the Land Beyond the Big Tunnel. Let's go directly to the camp leader's tipi and tell him what we have seen on our journey. We left here early in the summer and now it is fall here!" They went on travelling until they saw their old camp; but no one seemed to there. They saw that there was a trail leading out from the camp and they decided to follow that trail.

"Hey, we are out of food now," said the chief. "We better go and kill a deer." They went over the mountain and killed a fat buck deer, skinned it, cooked it and ate until they were satisfied. Then they packed the remaining pieces in their rawhide bags. They started on their journey once more. They stopped at nightfall and ate their supper, then they all went to sleep.

Their camp was situated on the top of a mountain, and when daybreak came they could see all over the country around them. Early in the morning one of thcm woke up and said, "I see a big smoke fog in that cottonwood down there in the valley. I wonder if it is our people's camp. You look down there and see if I am right." The others did so and said, "Yes, you are right and the smoke is getting thicker all the time." The chief said, "Let's go there when it gets dark so they can put up the council tipi."

They moved on then and walked and walked so that they arrived close to the camp around sundown. The chief said, "Now, let us comb our hair, paint ourselves up, shine up our necklaces and put on our buckskin suits and good moccasins." They did as he had suggested and went down to the camp leader's tipi. The camp leader said, "Come in, who are you? Aren't you the four boys who went off early in the spring?" "Yes," they answered. "Where have you been all this time?" asked the camp leader.

"Well," said their chief, "when we left here we went south and went into a tunnel which took us through a mountain. We had no food or water and no light there and it took two days and one night to walk through. Finally, we came out into a shining country, and we were pretty hungry. Then we came to a river and there was a big camp there, and the people spoke our language." "Do you know any of their names?" asked the camp leader. "No," replied the chief, "we didn't even ask what tribe they belonged to. They sleep during the daytime and have games of all kinds during the night. We will tell you the rest tomorrow morning." The camp leader said, "Get the chief announcer! I want him to announce that we will all hear the news about your journey tomorrow. Everybody will come here to hear it." The next morning the four travellers told the people their story. They all understood that those who lived on the other side of the tunnel were the people living in the realm of the dead![5]

Good Spirits, Helping Spirits

John Trehero said that "bear medicine is the strongest medicine that you can get, next to lightening *puha.* When you have a 'lightning dream', you see a bluish light. The lightning doesn't go downwards as when you are awake, it comes straight at you. A person who has been hit is thrown into the water, if he is badly burnt. There were two white boys in a wagon who were hit; one of them was killed, the other was burnt on his right side. The lightning had gone down from the head to the arm on the right side of the body and then also through the right leg. That boy survived though."

"All powers are good for sickness," said John. Every kind of *puha* can, on the one hand give enormous power, but on the other hand it can give limited power. An example of this is Norman's running medicine. *Puha* can differentiate as medicine for illnesses so that one can be stronger than the other. There are different levels of strength. "Just like *puha* going to school." It gets stronger as more is learned. The different levels are: from the top, with the exception of *PúhanpaBi:*
1. Lightning medicine – *Eygagú?ce:?puha* – good for rheumatism and more.
2. Bear medicine – *Agua?puha* – good for fever and measles.
3. Eagle medicine – *Pía guína puha* – if you are sleepy, tired and have difficulty in sleeping.
4. Beaver medicine – *Kastó:n puha* – good for rheumatism and all kinds of illnesses,
5. Buffalo medicine – *Kúcunand puha* – good for measles and smallpox.
6. Otter medicine – *Pandzú:k puha* good for illness.
7. Antelope medicine – *Gó:hǎri? Puha* – good as running medicine.

But there is an even stronger *puha* that John did not have, and that is at the sites of rock drawings, "the same spirit gives you all, takes care of all of it: *PúhanbaBi,* the Great Spirit." John said that we don't know who he is. "Might be Jesus, that's what some of them say. Some people call him *Dam Apö.* Some of them get *puha* from him, but I got mine from the mountains. Those who receive such *puha* never see the person, ´only fire.'" John mentioned that he had only known one man who had owned that kind of *puha,* but he had died. He had a very good reputation for curing the sick. "That had been the Holy Spirit, the strongest medicine.[6] *PúhanpaBi* is the leader of the spirits," just as the Chief is the head of the tribe. *PúhanpaBi* made the rock drawings at Dinwoody and many other places. He pecked them, and He has given them all their power – *puha.* "

"The best way to get *puha* is to ask for the lowest one, the Antelope." Said John Trehero. [Åke Hultkrantz asked at this point] If one could pray to the drawing of the Sun Dance figure at Dinwoody? "Of course," replied John;

117

"but he only gives you the order to put up a Sun Dance. You start with low medicine and advance upwards; even the Otter may start you out," *pandzú:k.* "The Antelope started me out," said John. "He turned me to a little baby to use *puha* on him."

John also had beaver *puha*, and at first he said that he couldn't remember how he got it, but then suddenly he came upon it. "*Pía guína* said to me in a dream, 'you should never want to eat beaver meat; some day you might get some *puha* from the beaver, if you stay with what I tell you.' It came to me: I dreamed about the beaver, I kept dreaming about him every now and then. Finally he told me how to use his power. The beaver said, 'here is my power,' and he showed me his front paws. This *puha* is very strong and powerful. If a person has a pain, I can put my hand on him and that pain comes into my hand. I use my own hands for beaver paws."

John went on, "*puha* has power over all, just like steam coming out of a teapot; but you don't see that teapot, just the steam when the *puha* is working right. Power isn't anything that is fixed: Power is like quicksilver: you can't hold it, still it's there to talk to you. Power is not an immovable thing, but it can have influence on a stone. *Tïmbimpuhagant* is the name of a medicine man with a holy stone. But: *Puha* is no dead thing, he has motion in him; sometimes he looks like a butterfly. Anyone of the high *puha* can send butterflies to you, or spirits who have wings like butterflies and hooks on their toes."

Spirits can thus send out other spirits; "one *puha* gets power from another, for example; the otter from the beaver, the beaver from lightning. The thunderbird is thunder *puha;* therefore thunder and the eagle are not the same thing." And at this point John maintained that he wasn't sure that the thunderbird was either the thunder or the eagle. However lightning and thunder are the same things as lightning is always followed by thunder. Thunder gets its power from the lightning.

John went on to say how he got other *puha.* "I got other medicine after antelope and other *puha;* then I jumped a few others; then I got Eagle medicine. Right now I have the highest *puha*, but not *PúhanpaBi.*"[7]

John said "all spirits are different," and not identical. The Bear Spirit looks like a bear, but differs from a real bear by appearing and disappearing suddenly. He is like a shadow, *hïgiexn.* "It has a bear form but is a spirit." Why just a bear form? "Well," answered John, "The Creator made him that way. The spirits have generations just like we do." John was also adamant that in no way had the Bear Spirit anything to do with a genuine bear or other bears.

No one here has bear *puha,* "he is too mean. I am afraid that I would have no friends if I had bear *puha*. You can draw bear *puha* from people, but you can't draw eagle power - *pía guina puha* or lightning power – *eygagú?ce:? puha,* nor otter, or elk; they are too strong. But you can draw bear *puha* and bird *puha*."

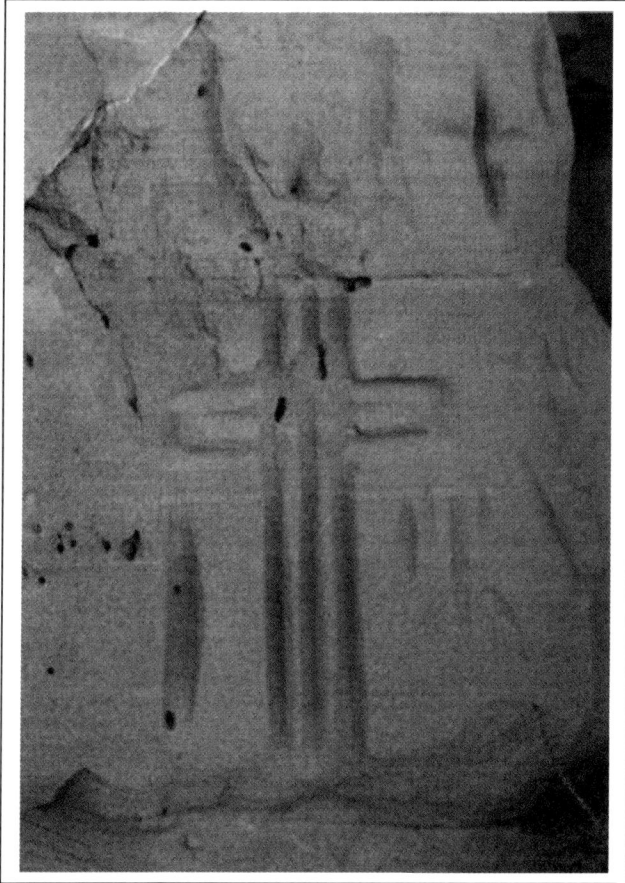

Concerning the Great Spirit – *Dam apö,* John said that "some claim that they have seen him like a fire, others claim that they have seen him in the form of a bird." In the earlier case there were some warriors who went on a war party. They saw a burning bush on the path, "The fire was there, but it didn't burn the brush; what they say was *Dam apö mugua,* our father's spirit. The fire told them: you're going to have bad luck, go back home."[8]

On another occasion God appeared as a bird, and "The bird told them: go back home and stay there, you are going to have bad luck."

John said that he could make out the difference between power dreams and ordinary dreams: if he saw lightning – *eygagú?ce:?,* first in the dream, then it was a power dream. If the dream was of thunder then it was also a power dream.

Love *Puha* – Medicine

If a man has love *puha*, then he is called a *waípepuhagant,* but a woman is called a *tïnapöpuhagant.* The persons who have this *puha* "can make you come close, they draw you with their power. The one who gives the client the love medicine is the love spirit; maybe you dream about some good looking girl, that's the *puha.* But I don't want the girl *puha*, I might do wrong with it, maybe the girl *puha* tells you something wrong, you perhaps get interested in a married woman!"

A plant called *Távemuzu?pi,* was used for love medicine. It grew on the hills, especially up at the rock drawings at North Popoagie. According to John Trehero. "It looks like the Morning Glory plant and has purple-pink-blue-reddish-yellow flowers and long, slim leaves. It is a spirit-like plant, but not as strong as *Tóyanatïwura,* (Mountain Medicine), that is also used as a love medicine. The flower blooms every morning at ten o'clock, but wilts in the evening. At sundown it looks as if it is just dying off. If you want to use it as love medicine, then you should pick it at sundown. You mustn't fool with it when it is awake. If a man puts it on the back of a girl she will become madly in love with him. One can even turn a girl's heart by sending her this flower attached to a present!"

Notes:

1. John Trehero told Åke Hultkrantz that he was afraid to take part in such competitions because he said, "I might lose my *puha.*"
2. *Tú:kuyuiki* can also mean a "bad look," "magician," " sorcery," or "sorcerer." This man can shoot you with his medicine. "He blows it on you," he can shoot something into you so that you feel sick the next morning. Another medicine man can find out who the guilty one is and can take the bad medicine man's medicine away from him. Such a sorcerer has only bad medicine. For example, *nïnïmbi puha.* One can take the medicine from such a man by putting a hand on his back and pulling out the medicine. Only another medicine man is able to do that. A very evil sorcerer who lived at the beginning of the reservation was *Óharu?tzi?* ("cross the river from here"). He had gopher medicine. He could often be seen to point a clenched hand at someone and blow towards that person. It is said that "They took the medicine away from him, and it turned against him, and he died."
3. The description here reminds us of the conception of the devil among Western people.
4. Please refer to Note 2.
5. There is the parallel among Western societies of "near death" experiences when the person in question travels through what seems to be a tunnel with a bright light at the end.
6. This reminds us of the "Miracle at Whitsuntide," the Holy Spirit as Fire.
7. This account differs slightly from other accounts that John Trehero related to Åke.
8. Åke Hultkrantz asked here about the resemblance to the story of "the burning bush" in the Bible, but John Trehero denied that it had any connection with that.

Final Observations

A.K and Geraldine have studied the Shoshone Stories and have been struck with many likenesses to the fairy-Stories that are part of many other cultures. (e.g. coyote in some stories is rather like the wolf in "Little Red Riding Hood.") In the story where the young man fights the dragon to win the hand of the princess we can see a similarity to the story of "St. George and the Dragon:" I am sure that the reader will agree that many of these stories have parallels in other cultures all over the world. It is also good to find the things which are unique to the Wind River Reservation peoples, and enjoy those points of view which are demonstrated in these writings. Sincerely, Geraldine Hultkrantz.